Unraveling:
The New World
Part One

C. JANE REID

FICSTITCHES YARNS KIT CLUB

Every craft lovingly handmade tells a story. Ficstitches Yarns takes creating to another level by offering crochet patterns along with hand-dyed yarns, handmade accessories and hooks, and fictional stories, all bound together in a theme of romance, history, the coming-together of friends, and a touch of magic. Thank you for joining us on our fiber adventure.

ACKNOWLEDGMENTS

This book wouldn't be in existence without the brilliant creative genius of Laurinda Reddig. Thank you for dragging me into this. Thanks also goes to Monica Lowe for the marvelous way she made Elsie's shawl pin come to life. Thanks to all of my beta readers for their insights and catching my typos, to Caren Lee for her fine proofreading and for the use of her floor, and to my family for allowing me to disappear into the 1720s for hours at a time. And a special thanks to Mom, who both encourages me and helps me to see all the practical angles at the same time.

CHAPTER ONE

September 11th, 1720
Londonderry, Ireland

Of all the places I thought I might one day find myself, a dock in Londonderry had never crossed my mind. I belonged nowhere near a ship. Yet here I stood dressed in my second-best skirt and bodice amidst the rank stench of the docks, all my worldly belongings packed in crates about me. And not many crates, either. No, I'd given away as many things as I'd been allowed to bring.

Still, I smiled to myself. I'd hidden the shawl my mother had given me on my wedding day. Grahame thought I'd given it to the Karney girl, but I couldn't bring myself to do it. I gave the girl my nicest stays instead. They were only good to wear to church, as the boning pinched too much for everyday work. She wouldn't find any use for it, except to reuse the linen and boning, but at least she could do that much. I was still learning my stitches.

I shifted on my feet, holding my canvas bag closer. A couple of men ambled past, sailors by the look at them, with rough shorn hair and patched clothes and a strange swagger in their walk. I half-expected them to say something, or at least look at me, a young woman standing alone in the early morning amid crates at the side of the dock, but they passed without a glance. Was it so common to see a young woman waiting on the docks?

I wasn't the only woman at the dockside, though—just the only one standing alone. The other passengers were gathered several paces away. The women were keeping an eye on a handful of children while the men stood nearby, watchful.

Grahame was speaking with two other men by the pier in the shadow of a tall, three-masted ship. One of them was the captain. The second man looked to be the leader of the group. I couldn't hear them speaking, and I didn't know the man I'd married well enough to read his stance. The other two men looked relaxed, though, and welcoming.

The other passengers clearly knew one another. I tried not to stare but stole quick glances instead to examine them. I didn't recognize any of the women. That was a blessing at least. I couldn't bear to spend however long we were going to be on a ship pretending not to hear remarks made about me.

Perhaps Mother had been right and this was the chance at a new beginning. I had a new husband taking me to a new land for a new start at life without the mistakes of the past dogging my steps.

I stood straighter and lifted my chin. I could pretend this was good and try to ignore the sinking feeling in my stomach.

Grahame looked in my direction, and I was pleased to think that I might look confident and ready for whatever the future held. I wished I could read his expression better, but his dark eyes kept his secrets too well. It gave me pause to realize how untamed he looked. Grahame was presentable, his coat and trousers clean and well-mended, his black hair drawn back, and his beard trimmed. The leader, however, wore a powdered wig that was the current fashion, and his coat and knee breeches were tailored. He was shorter than Grahame by at least a hand-span and a bit portly around the middle. Grahame was long and lean, and when he moved, it was like watching a wolfhound on the prowl.

The captain turned for his ship, and Grahame and the second man came towards me. I tried to keep my expression polite, but my heart was hammering.

"Mr. Vance," Grahame said by way of introduction. "My wife, Ailee." His tone was neutral, as though he wasn't certain how to feel yet about having a wife.

"Mrs. Donaghue," the man said politely. I inclined my head, not sure if I should bend a knee or not.

"What fortune to have taken such a comely young wife, Mr. Donaghue," Mr. Vance said to Grahame. I struggled to keep my own expression smooth. Of course that was what Mr. Vance would see—a young woman not yet twenty wooed and won by a man ten years her senior. I should have been thankful that's all he saw and not the truth behind it.

I hid my thoughts behind as calm an expression as I could manage, thankful that I did when Grahame glanced at me. His own look was still unreadable.

"Shall we settle the terms with the captain while the crates are loaded?" Mr. Vance gestured toward the ship. "Your young wife can stay with our women. She'll be made welcome."

"Fine." A typical one-word answer from Grahame.

Mr. Vance raised his hand toward the women, and one broke free of the group to join them. "My wife, Tavey Vance," he told me. "She'll help you see to what you need."

The men left us to glance over each other. The older woman was dressed in clothing that had been mended a few times, with touches of lace on her mobcap and on the kerchief around her neck. Her shawl was knitted wool. She was neither stout nor frail, and I guessed her age a couple decades above my own. Her face had fine lines that suggested she smiled often, though at the moment she was appraising me with a solemn expression. Despite my finer clothing, I felt sized up and found lacking.

"Have you a name, child?"

"Ailee."

"And your family?"

"Only my husband," I answered, feeling a pang at the lie. But it was also the truth. I'd left home and family behind.

A new beginning, Mother had said. Mother wasn't the one leaving everything she'd ever known.

"Well then, let's see if you're prepared." The woman held out her hand. With a start, I realized Mrs. Vance wanted to see what I carried. I considered refusing, but then I wasn't entirely certain what I did need. Grahame had seen to all of our supplies except for my own possessions, and he'd merely limited me in the number of items with a few curt suggestions I hadn't dared refuse. Except for the shawl, which I'd hidden in my bag. The bag Mrs. Vance held out her hand to take.

"Oh, come now, child," Mrs. Vance said in a tone my mother used with the serving girl. "Once you're on the ship, there'll be no chance to fetch what you might be missing."

Suppressing a sigh, I handed over the bag. Mrs. Vance untied the knots with deft fingers. "Let's see then," she said, and she laid out my things across the top of the nearest crate, saying each item as though ticking them off a list. "Your huswife and apron, stockings and kerchief, comb and brush, a mirror, my that is fancy now isn't it, wool and needles, haven't gotten far on this knitting have you, gloves, not sure you'll be needing these, but they're small enough, and—what's this?"

Mrs. Vance held up the shawl. It was a triangle of finely woven ivory linen with cheyne lace in pale thread worked around the edges and three large cheyne lace flowers attached at the mid-points. Mrs. Vance gave me a long look. Wordlessly, she folded the shawl and put it back in the bag, replacing all the rest with it except the wool and needles. She pulled the needles free of the ball of wool and stretched them out to see the strip of knitting I had managed.

I heard the women tsk under her breath. "We'll need to work on this," she said in a kinder tone. "You've dropped stitches, I can see, but there's a trick to picking them up. We've plenty of time to have it finished before we make land."

I nodded, my throat thick.

Mrs. Vance eyed me. "How long since you wed?"

"Just last month."

"Do you think you are with child?"

I felt my face burn and shook my head.

"Sure, are you? Good, that's good. Two of our women are carrying, God help them, and it'll make the crossing all the worse. Been aboard ship before?"

I shook my head.

"'Tisn't so bad if you've the stomach for it, I'm told" Mrs. Vance said sagely. "Jacky," she called to the group, her voice piercing through the noise of the docks. One of the men hurried over to her. He was tall, nearly as tall as Grahame, but gangly, like he hadn't quite finished growing. He looked around my age or maybe in his early twenties, and he wore a friendly smile. He moved as though he wasn't quite comfortable in his short breeches and buckled shoes, as if he'd have been more at ease in a kilt and boots.

"Fetch some of those boys," Mrs. Vance instructed to him, "and have them move these crates over to ours. Mrs. Donaghue and her husband will be joining us for the crossing. You come with me, Ailee, and meet the others."

Swept up in the woman's wake, I could do nothing but follow, uncertain what had just happened. I'd gone from suspicious to pitiable in the space of a moment. What had Mrs. Vance thought of the shawl? It was a useless thing, I knew. All lace and frail linen, meant for show and splendor. I'd been so proud of myself, hiding a bit of culture from my old life to carry into my new, a piece of my old identity to remind myself that once I'd been well-to-do and admired.

Now I was simply ashamed of it. I should have given it to the Karney girl.

At least I had my everyday shawl. It was warm and sturdy and everything a women like Mrs. Vance must admire. Mother had tutted at it, and I had worn it each day with a sense of dismay ever since the Karney girl had given it to me, but now I was happy to have it. Especially when Mrs. Vance introduced me to another young woman who wore a similarly worked shawl.

"Elsie, this is Ailee. She and her husband will be crossing with us."

Elsie, a fair girl with warm brown eyes and a ready smile, looked close to my age, too. Her dress was plainer than Mrs. Vance's, though she wore a bit of cheyne lace on the kerchief at her throat. I had the impression that everyone in the group was dressed in their finest clothing. Which put them a bit richer than Grahame, but not by much, and certainly nowhere near my parents' standing.

"Elsie MacClayne," she introduced herself. "So pleased to meet you, Ailee. Did you travel far?"

"A seven-day," I said.

"Are those your livestock?" another woman asked, gesturing toward the small, fenced yard across the road. "I saw your man with them earlier."

"We should have brought livestock," a second woman said.

"Bruce says there'll be plenty for purchase after we cross," answered the first woman.

"From where?" I asked before I thought better of it.

"The town, naturally." The first woman answered as though speaking to a young, rather slow-witted child. My cheeks burned.

"Be kind, Iona," Elsie said. "We've all wondered, too, what might be there."

I couldn't picture a town, such as where I stood, existing across the sea in a wilderness of no real country. I wasn't well-traveled, not like some of the folks my parents had entertained, but I'd grown up in Lifford, and I'd visited Letterkenny once when I was much younger. I recalled being overwhelmed by the number of buildings and people the city held. Londonderry was probably as large, or larger, and I'd been a bit overwhelmed entering it yesterday. These cities had been founded generations ago. The new world wasn't even a proper country, so how could it have towns?

"Fine looking sheep," Mrs. Vance said. "I hope we won't have to eat them."

I started at the comment. Why would we want to eat the sheep? That's what the chickens were for.

"How many hens have you?" Elsie asked as if reading my thoughts. "We brought about twenty, but three stopped laying."

"Fifteen," I answered. I had no idea which were laying or not. I'd only recently learned how to care for them and had the peck marks to show it.

"I wonder where they'll put all this stuff," the second woman said. "And the animals. They won't like being in the ship's belly."

"Better than in ours." The woman, Iona, laughed at her own jest. She was a large woman with lace around her mob cap and a mole like a lump of dirt on her chin. She had a coarse voice, like she'd been yelling at the children.

Elsie pulled me a few steps away from the others. "Don't mind Iona. She doesn't like the thought of sea travel, and she's loud when she's nervous. She's a wonderful cook and so handy with a needle. Not as good as Tavey, though. How are your stitches?"

"Sturdy," I answered. "According to my husband." Truly, though, it is the only kind thing one could say about my needlework. I had never had a fair hand for it. And I wondered why Elsie asked it of me. It was a strange way to start a friendship. The Karney girl had done much the same, as though all wives and wives-to-be should talk of needlework.

"I do so like stitching, though I'm better at knitting."

"I'm hopeless at knitting," I admitted.

"This is very finely done," Elsie told me, touching the shawl I wore.

"It was a neighbor's work. She was trying to teach me, but I can't get the needles to work the way I wish."

"Only just learning?" Elsie sounded surprised.

I avoided answering. "I'm fair at spinning, though. I packed my wheel."

"Did you? Jacky promised to make me a new one when we arrived. I gave mine to one of the local girls."

"You couldn't bring it?"

"We're so limited on what we could pack—Jacky had tools he needed to bring instead."

"Why though?" I asked, finally giving voice to thoughts that had nagged at me since leaving the village. "It's a big enough ship. Seems as though we could have a bit more room for our things."

"I think it is something to do with the weight. Jacky tried to explain it. He's in love with the idea of sailing. The only thing I could liken it to was over-filling a cart."

"But a ship has no axle. And it can't bog in the mud."

"But it can sink," Iona interrupted loudly. "And it could founder."

"Let's not be having talk of sinking," Tavey told me. "Not before we're to board."

There wasn't much to do on the dock. I stayed near Elsie, and we helped watch the children. There were eight, ranging in age of a couple of years to ten. There was a babe, too, tied by a shawl to a nervous-looking mother with red-rimmed eyes. I learned through a few questions to Elsie and listening to the talk around me that the members of the group were all from the same village. There were nearly ninety of them, and this voyage had been over a year in the planning. A couple of families had already made the crossing, and the news from them had been good. They all hoped to meet again in the new world.

"Have you family there?" Elsie asked.

"My husband does. His brother. And an uncle, I think, or an aunt. But I don't, myself."

"My cousin went," Elsie told me. "I had a letter from him a few months back. He says it is amazing there. A little frightening at times, but like a paradise."

I smiled but kept my thoughts to myself. Grahame didn't act like it was paradise. He'd crated his guns and powder and sword while I'd watched, wide-eyed and chilled. I heard him tell the Karney girl's father that it was an opportunity for the bold.

I was raised to be confident, perhaps even bold, but my nature was far more daring than a young lady's should be, or so my mother had often commented. I'd been daring once, against all propriety. It had cost me everything. I didn't intend to make that mistake again.

The men joined us, Grahame among them. He came over and gave me that questioning look I'd finally interpreted as his way of asking if all was well. I gave him a brief nod, which seemed to please him. He wasn't one for words, my husband. I was learning.

"We'll board as soon as the supplies are settled," Mr. Vance told everyone. "It shouldn't take too long. Keep close to the ship, though. The captain means to leave on time, and I doubt he'll wait for anyone who strays."

I looked to Grahame, not sure where to go.

"The livestock," Grahame told me in that quiet way of his. I suppressed a sigh, knowing I wouldn't be of much use, but I followed him across the road to the stockyard.

I was surprised when, after he closed the gate and we were among the sheep, he spoke. "Were they friendly?"

The women, he meant. With a start I realized that he'd sent me among them to sound out the group. Clever, though I wished he'd warned me. I suppose he might fear I'd give it away, though I'd think he'd have learned I could keep a secret when needed.

"Yes. They're all of the same village, following a few families who've already crossed. Elsie said the rents had gone up again across the village, and their flax crop failed for the second year. Several of their herds got the rot, too."

Grahame was going from sheep to sheep, checking them over. "I heard the same."

"They admired your herd," I told him. My voice went all quiet and breathy for some reason.

He glanced over at me. I thought I saw the shadow of a smile cross his face, but it might have been a trick of the sunlight. "Have they any livestock?"

"Chickens. A few milk cows." I was surprised by how much I'd learned listening to the women talk. "I brought the shawl," I added impulsively.

Grahame straightened, a questioning look crossing his eyes.

"The lace shawl," I told him. "The one I said I gave to the Karney girl. I kept it. I am sorry." I didn't know why I felt compelled to apologize. It was my shawl.

It wasn't about the shawl, I realized. I didn't want falsehoods between us. Grahame and I had enough between us as it was, and I'd had enough of

7

lies to last a lifetime.

Grahame was silent for a moment. "It's fine," he said at last.

I drew a shuddering breath. "It is?"

This time the smile wasn't a shadow. "Yes."

He'd known all along. He'd been waiting for me to tell him. "I'm sorry," I said again, but not for the shawl.

He touched my cheek, gently, something he hadn't done before. "Thank you."

I wanted to step into the circle of his arms, but I didn't dare. He was still a stranger, no matter that we'd shared a bed. So I offered him a smile instead.

"How can I help?" I asked.

"The chickens."

That, at least, I knew how to do.

CHAPTER TWO

The *Resolution* was a tall ship with three masts and two raised decks, fore and aft. "That's the forecastle," Jacky told Elsie as the last of the crates was being loaded. I stood nearby, watching the couple but trying not to do so obviously. Jacky was dripping sweat from helping haul, and his lank brown hair was sodden and hung clinging to the sides of his face where it had come loose from the binding. Elsie's whole bearing had changed when he'd joined her, becoming relaxed and content, like a cat curled before a fire.

"And that's the quarter deck," Jacky continued. "And the fore and main and mizzen masts. They'll have gun decks, too, I expect."

"And a kitchen, I hope," Elsie said with a fond grin for her husband.

"Galley," he corrected. "Yes, but small."

"And rooms for us all?"

Jacky gave her a smile. "No rooms. Berths."

"Oh dear, that doesn't sound pleasant."

"It'll be fine," he told her. "You'll see. Close, but we're all friends and family." His easy grin took in me as well. "Your man knows his way about a ship, I noticed. Done much sailing, has he?"

"I couldn't say," I admitted, a bit startled. Grahame had not spoken of any time at sea. Then again, he'd not spoken much of his life before I came into it. I'd have never taken him for a sailor, though.

"He won't care for his height below decks," Jacky said. "I walloped my head twice now." He rivaled Grahame in height, though he was as slender as a reed.

"Mind yourself," Elsie told him. "You can't afford to be shaking loose any of the sense that remains to you."

They chuckled, and I joined in. I was growing fond of the couple. We were close in age, if not experience. Jacky looked as though he'd never said a cross word in his life, and Elsie had such a gentle and welcoming manner that I couldn't help but to want to like her. They were unlike any one I'd called friend before. That was a small blessing.

Grahame joined us, looking none the worse for having helped load. "It's time," he told me.

"What about the animals?"

"They load after the women and children."

"The captain will want the ship ready to sail," Jacky added, "before the decks are crowded with beasts."

"They'll stay on the decks?" I was shocked at the thought.

"There's a place in the hold for the chickens," Jacky assured me. "And a few bits and crannies should the weather turn, but mostly they'll be topside."

"They'll be fine," Grahame said. "Come."

I picked up my bag and followed my husband toward the ship, Elsie and Jacky trailing after. The hull of the ship towered over me as I approached the plank that led up to its deck. It heaved with the warp and weave of the water, dipping down and then riding high. The plank was wide, but without rails or even ropes to grasp, nothing would keep me from pitching into the water between the dock and the ship should I misstep.

Grahame must have noticed my hesitation. "I'll be right behind you," he said, bending low to speak in my ear. His nearness was both foreign and comforting.

Grasping my bag close, I stepped onto the plank. It felt stable and stout, so I took another step. I could sense Grahame and his steadying presence behind me. The ship raised, and the plank with it. For a moment I thought I would fall, but I kept my balance. The ship settled and butterflies chased around in my belly. I laughed louder than I should have, but the sensation was so thrilling, a mixture of fear and excitement that left me breathless.

"See, Elsie," I heard Jacky say from the dock, "there's nothing to it. No need for nerves, my lass."

I crossed the rest of the length and stepped down onto the deck. I nearly skipped with pride. I found Grahame watching me and was surprised to see a gleam of pleasure in his eyes.

Jacky guided Elsie across, holding her hand until they reached the ship and then lifting her down to the deck. Elsie was pale, but she tried for a wan smile to her husband.

The deck was thick with sailors and passengers. Men were leading the women and children through a narrow doorway set in the wall of the quarter deck as sailors scurried up masts and across yardarms, working with the ropes tying down the sails. Jacky was caught up watching the sailors, but Grahame ignored the bustle and led me to the door, gesturing inside.

The passage was narrow with a low ceiling and smelt of sweat, tar, and dampness with a pungent under-scent I couldn't place. We had to wait for the line of passengers to file down a sturdy but steep set of stairs. The children seemed thrilled and called out with shrieks and laughter. The women muttered about the closeness.

Two decks down, a long, low-ceilinged hallway spanned half the length of the ship. On one side hung cots one above another—not proper beds but these things made of canvas hanging between the beams with rope. No bedding, either. Oil lamps hung along the other wall, carefully shielded to keep the flames protected. Their light managed to cast more gloom than true illumination. It was like entering a wooden cavern and it felt confining and depressing. I heard one woman liken it to moving into a root cellar.

"We're at the far end," Grahame told me, his voice low in my ear. His breath across my neck chased an unexpected thrill up my spine, and I could feel the warmth of him against my back. We'd spent the last month alone together on his farm with only our wedding night shared between us. Why was I having these sensations now?

The last two cots hung at the far end of the berths near the opening to another passage. Steps branched from the passage, but where the steps led, I couldn't say. The rank stench was worse at this end. It seems that being made welcome by the group didn't give us the option for a better position in the berths, but the worst of it.

"What is that smell?" I finally asked.

"Fish," Grahame answered. "A shipment went bad. It will pass."

Please, God, let it be so, I prayed, but I was dubious. My stomach knotted from the overpowering stench.

Grahame had been busy as a few of our boxes and bags were waiting for us. The boxes were tied to the beams and the bags hung from pegs. He had already assembled one of the small wooden stools he had dismantled and packed before our journey from the farm, a thoughtful gesture towards my comfort as there were no other seats in sight.

Grahame moved to one of the boxes, pulling out blankets for us both. "You have the top cot. The stool will help you. I'll help, too, if it's needed," he added as a look of doubt that crossed my face.

I glanced around. "Are there no rooms? For changing and the like?"

"We'll hang a blanket," he said.

The truth about what this voyage would be like began to dawn on me. The farmhouse had been small, much smaller than I was accustomed to, but Grahame had respected my privacy. On the ship, however, I would be cramped with over ninety strangers, including a husband I was only beginning to get to know, on decks that reeked of fish, with all my worldly possessions tied in a bag to the wall, for several weeks while we journeyed across the sea. Desperation hit me with such force, I had to grasp the cot to steady myself. The material was rough and unforgiving. Like this ship. Like my new life.

—" Grahame reached for me, his tone odd. He took gentle hold
⸗m.

⸗orced myself upright and took a deep breath, but the stench choked
⸗fforts.

"We can go on the deck, can't we?" I asked with a note of pleading I
couldn't suppress. "During the voyage?"

"When it's safe." He looked uncertain, as if wondering if I were going to
faint. I tried to gather myself once more.

"Good. That's good." I struggled to regain some semblance of
composure.

"Ailee," he said again, stepping closer. He took hold of my other arm.
With gentle pressure, he pulled me against his chest. My heart thudded, and
with a swift burning of tears, I buried my face against him. I blinked
furiously to keep from crying.

He didn't offer me a word, simply held me until I had control. I pushed
against him and he released me.

"I need to check the livestock," he told me, uncertainty in his voice.

"Of course." I raised my face to show him that I was recovered. I didn't
try to smile. I knew it would look sick and pathetic. He waited another
moment, as if to give me a chance to change my mind, then left through the
passage next to us.

I busied myself to keep the anxiety at bay, poking through the boxes and
bags. Clothes, soap, eating and cooking utensils, stores of food, a few extra
blankets, and, oddly, my spinning wheel.

"It's dreadful, isn't it," I heard Elsie say. I stood to see my new friend
poking at the cots. "I don't know how I'll sleep in such things."

"I don't know how to even get into it," I said, trying to keep my tone
light. Elsie made a small laugh, but it sounded forced. "I suspect we'll
adjust," I told her. "Maybe in a few weeks, it'll be like we've always slept
this way."

"Weeks." Elsie wrapped her arms around herself. "I don't think I can do
it."

I moved over to her and put an arm around her after a moment's
hesitation. "I'll help you," I said, wondering how I intended to do such a
thing. "We'll help each other."

Elsie leaned her head on my shoulder in a way no other person had
done before. A fierce protectiveness swelled in me.

"We can do this," I whispered, for both our sakes.

I wanted to be on deck when the ship left port, but Grahame told me it
would be too crowded. So Elsie and I sat together on Grahame's cot, our
feet planted on the worn wood decking to keep the cot from swinging. The

other women did the same, sitting on cots or on stools they'd brought with them, minding the children who were occupying themselves by racing up and down the passage. The air was still pungent, with oil lamps adding a haziness to the air and casting deep shadows, but it was cozy in a strange way. I had a feeling the coziness would soon turn to confinement.

The motion of the ship changed slightly as we left dock, but not extremely so. The cot tried to swing out a couple of times, but Elsie and I held it still. We didn't speak to one another, both pretending to work on our knitting, though our needles lay mostly quiet. We glanced upwards from time to time, as though we might be able to tell what was happening by the look of the planks above our heads.

"I don't see why the men should be topside," Iona was complaining not far from us. "It's not like they have a lick of sense about sailing. What one of them has ever been on a ship before? And what if they catch chill? We'll be the ones caring for them."

"You know how the men get about these things," Mrs. Vance told her. "They'll come down after we've set off."

I didn't hear Iona's reply. What were we going to do for weeks stuck aboard a ship? Knitting for the women, I imagined. Or sewing or embroidery. And the men . . . they might get to learn a thing or two about sailing. Put them to work topside. Wouldn't the sailors be angry if the men sat around while there was work to be done? Or would they prefer strangers keep below and out of the way?

Questions I'd never thought to ask danced around my head. Weeks. In here. With these people. Listening to Iona scoff and Mrs. Vance placate and the children shriek and—

"Those must be dark thoughts you're thinking," Elsie said.

I had to laugh. "Yes, I guess they were."

"What shall we do instead?"

"I don't know. I do wish we could be on deck." I glanced upwards again, but the wood planks told me nothing.

"Jacky says they'll let us up once we're in the lough. You have your knitting." Elsie nodded toward the ladies nearby who were occupying themselves with their needles. Mine were laying forgotten in my lap.

I let out a long sigh. "Yes."

"You don't care much for it, do you?"

"No, well, not exactly," I answered. "I'm just so awful at it all."

"I'm surprised your mother did not force you to practice. Mine was strict about it."

I thought about shying away from the comment, but I wanted to trust Elsie. "Mother thought embroidery more suitable," I told her.

Elsie's mouth opened in surprise, but she closed it quickly.

"I am trying to learn, though," I continued. "If you might have any suggestions?"

"Practice," Elsie said firmly.

We were at it for some while, working on the shawl I had begun under the Karney girl's instruction. Elsie made suggestions and showed me when I'd dropped a stitch or added an extra. I was relieved when Jacky came for us. My eyes were strained from trying to see the stitches in the gloomy light, and my jaw ached from clenching it in concentration.

"Do you want to go topside?" Jacky asked. "Your man said it was fine," he added with a look to me.

I nodded eagerly. Elsie seemed less inclined, but she let Jacky convince her. I shoved my knitting back into my bag, hung it on a peg, and followed Elsie and Jacky up the narrow steps.

The sunlight was bright enough to blind after spending time in the dark berths. The deck was busy with sailors, and there was a rhythm to their work that nearly matched the rhythmic swelling of the ship through the waters of Lough Foyle. Jacky led us around the sailors to where Grahame and Mr. Vance stood at the rail.

My husband offered me a slight smile as I joined him. He gestured to his place by the rail, and I stepped up. The breeze tugged at my mob cap, pulling a few locks of my auburn hair free to spill across my face and neck. The breeze felt glorious, clean and crisp and carrying the scent of damp earth and green growing things. The water splashed against the hull below me and the lough spread out around us until it spilled onto the rocky shore of Donegal county.

Sudden tears blurred my vision. This might be the last time I looked upon my homeland. Would I ever see Ireland again? What would the new land look like where we traveled? Could it ever be so green, so wild, so rich with history and tradition? Green, perhaps, and certainly wild, but how could a place so newly settled ever feel rich? I hadn't realized the intangible things I was losing.

I was clutching the rail, the polished wood strong and solid beneath my grip.

"'Tis a lovely way to say farewell," I heard Jacky say to Elsie.

I felt Grahame's hand on my shoulder. I looked up at him, but he was looking out over the waters of the lough, at the shore sliding past. His expression was closed, his gaze far away, as if he were seeing something beyond the shores. I wanted to ask him what he saw, but I hesitated to break into his reverie.

"This isn't so bad," Mr. Vance was saying to his wife, who had come topside with most of the other women. They were standing on the other side of Jacky and Elsie, staring out at the shore. "If the crossing is like this, we'll have an easy one."

I glanced at Jacky. Elsie was standing with her back against his chest, leaning into him, a hopeful smile on her face. Jacky, however, was looking down at her with apprehension.

What did he know that Mr. Vance didn't?

Grahame's hand tightened on my shoulder, drawing my attention. I found him also watching Elsie. He had the same look in his eye as Jacky.

Worry unsettled my stomach and I drew a step closer to him. His arm went around my shoulders and I welcomed his warmth and his closeness, foreign as it was. I wasn't alone. I might not know the people around me, but I wasn't alone.

CHAPTER THREE

I remained on the deck as the other women went back below. Standing by the rail out of the way of the crew, I tried to ignore the worry gnawing at me. Grahame left to help the sailors, and Jacky shadowed him, watching what he did. It was surprising to see how much Grahame understood ships and sailing. The captain commented on it as well, and I was close enough to overhear.

"You've seen a few ships in your day," the captain said.

"A few," Grahame agreed.

"Ever been across the Atlantic?"

"No, sir, nothing so grand."

"Even so," the captain said, "another steady hand is always welcome."

Where had he traveled, I wondered? I'd never asked him about his past. I hadn't the right given my own. But now I wished I knew. What little I had learned from the Karney girl was that he had left home at a young age after some disagreement with his father and had been gone ten years at least. He'd come home in time to make peace with the old man before he'd died and had then taken over the farming and the herds.

He seemed at ease on the ship, and he didn't seem to mind Jacky's attention. He didn't say much to the younger man, but he slowed his knot-tying to give Jacky a chance to see how it was done. I was less uneasy seeing how confident he was on a ship.

Before going below, Elsie had wandered over to see the animals in their rope enclosure by the forecastle. Altogether, there were a dozen sheep, most of them Grahame's, four milk cows, one of them Grahame's, and a bull, also Grahame's. The bull was gentle as a babe, something for which I was thankful, for he was a thick-horned, sturdy beast. The chickens were below. I wanted to see to them, but I hadn't been able to force myself back into the belly of the ship quite yet. It was so pleasant on the deck.

The ship itself had seemed large from the dock, but now aboard with easily the same number of sailors as passengers, it felt not nearly large enough. The masts, however, were as thick as tree trunks, wider around than I could circle my arms. The sails overhead were like canopies, flapping and billowing with the winds. But what was more amazing was how clean it all was. The decks were scrubbed, the brass polished, the inside of the railing was even painted a lovely shade of blue. This was a ship to be proud of and she was treated as such.

If only below-decks could be as clean.

Not that they were dirty, I reminded myself. They had been clean, just dark and smelly. But Grahame had said the smell would fade.

I joined Elsie by the sheep. The wind was still strong, even in the lee of the forecastle, and I had to clutch at my shawl to keep it from tugging free.

Elsie was stroking one of the sheep along the face. The touch seemed to bring both her and the animal comfort, but Elsie's expression was tight. The wind tugged at her mob cap and her shawl, but a clever curve of beaten copper wire kept her shawl in place.

"Is that a shawl pin?" I asked her.

Elsie put her hand to the pin and a smile brightened her face. "Of a sort. Jacky made it for me when we were courting. He was always teasing me for losing my shawl pins. The pins would work loose and fall before I knew it, and I never could find them again. So he made me this."

The pin was curled into a flattened spiral, with a sharpened end to slide into and around the stitches, gathering the layers together and holding them in place. It was very clever, and I could see how useful it would be.

"Does it leave holes?"

"Not too badly," Elsie said. Her expression grew pensive again. "We should go below," she said, glancing around the deck.

"I think Grahame would tell us if we needed to. Stay out a bit longer."

Elsie took a long breath, as though weighing the chance of catching a windborne illness versus the discomfort of the cramped, stinky berths below.

I understood how she felt. For most of my life I'd been warned about staying outside for too long and the dangers of catching a chill. Grahame insisted on being outside as much as possible, though. We had even taken meals at a table he'd set under the eaves of the farmhouse. He must have picked up the habit during his travels.

After a month with him, I had begun to understand. I felt so much more freedom being outside. So much more alive. The stench of chamber pots and smoke and old meals was oppressive when I went back inside. And here it was worse. "Do you think there's a way to air out the berths?"

Elsie laughed. "Wouldn't that be handy? But I suppose we could ask. Jacky might know. He's been learning all he can from whoever would speak to him of ships and sailing. We'll ask him at supper."

I frowned, stymied by another problem I hadn't considered. "What will supper be? Are we to cook it? Where would we cook it?"

"I'm not sure," Elsie admitted. "Let's find Tavey. She'll know, I'm certain."

Mrs. Vance had gone below, and I was loath to do so. But if I would be expected to supply a meal for Grahame and myself, I needed to figure out how and soon. The sun was riding high in the sky. It was well past time for the noon meal.

Reluctantly, I followed Elsie back into the ship. The smell was as bad as before, but now the odor of too many bodies in too close of space mingled with the stench of rotting fish.

We found Mrs. Vance helping hang blankets between cots to serve for a bit of privacy.

"All settled?" the older woman asked us.

"For now," Elsie answered. "We were wondering what to do about meals?"

"Bruce says there is a cook aboard," Mrs. Vance told us. A cook? Of course, that made sense. Someone would have to feed all those sailors. "No doubt he'll be of help. And we've plenty of fresh supplies to be used for the next few days. The captain has said cook fires are to be lit outside the kitchen."

Galley, I corrected, but silently.

"So we'll need to arrange the use of it," Mrs. Vance continued. "I was going to ask Iona to speak with the cook. Mr. Beacham is his name. He'll be a bit coarse, but I expect he'll mind his manners around ladies. Why don't you go with her?"

"Are you certain we should be the ones to go, Mrs. Vance?" I asked. I wasn't so sure how welcoming Iona would be of my company.

"I don't see why not," she told me. "And please, call me Tavey. It's a long voyage for such formality."

Elsie and I exchanged looks, uncertain. Tavey went back to her work, leaving us to find Iona.

"Let me speak with her," Elsie said. "She can be a bit harsh."

I'd already taken note of Iona's manner and had no trouble letting Elsie handle her.

We found her at the other end of the berths, chastising a pair of boys for going topside without their parents.

"And if I catch you at it again, I'll take a switch to your backsides," she finished. The boys were cowering. I figured them between eight and ten, brothers or cousins by the look of them. They scurried off to their cots when Iona turned away from them.

"Tavey thought we might accompany you to the galley," Elsie said in a sweet, placating tone.

Iona bristled. "I'll not set another foot into that man's kitchen, God save me. Have a go at me, will he? He'll be wishing he had our help when the time comes to feed us all."

Elsie and I exchanged looks once more.

"Does Tavey know—" Elsie began, but Iona cut her off.

"Tavey can go speak with him herself. I've other work to tend."

"And where," I ventured before the bitter woman could leave, "might Tavey find the cook?"

Iona waved toward the passageway we had first entered. "Up those stairs and through the first doorway and go to the end of the hall."

She turned away then.

Elsie bit her lip in chagrin as I stood staring the direction Iona had gestured. Going by ourselves hadn't been exactly what Tavey had meant, but Iona hadn't given us much choice.

"It can't be hard to find," I said. "We might have better luck than she."

Elsie hesitated.

I straightened my shoulders, determined to manage some part of this voyage on my own. "Shall we be at it?"

I thought Elsie might refuse, but apparently the idea of letting me go alone was too much. She nodded, though reluctantly.

We wended our way past the last few berths and mounted the stairs. The first passage was narrow and the roof came close to touching the tops of our caps. The entrance at the end of the hall opened to a narrow space crowded with a closed-in hearth, a board leveled along one angled wall with pots hanging from hooks over it, and shelves fronted with a plank to keep their contents from spilling free.

The thin man filling the narrow space turned to cast a fierce gaze upon us. He was an unkempt little man with an evil cast to his eye, his lank hair bound back by a stained kerchief, his clothing equally stained, though, I noted with dismay, well stitched.

"What do ye what?" His tone was hard, and he spoke in a Londoner's accent.

"We've come to offer a hand at meals?" I offered.

The man glared at me. "If I wanted women in my galley," he growled, "I'd have married and taken a house. Get out, the both of ye. I've no use fer the either of ye. 'Tis my duty to feed those souls aboard ship, and do that I will." His growl had twisted into a hissing lisp, as though he hadn't all his teeth.

Elsie backed away, frightened, but a stab of anger drove me to speak even when I knew it would be best to keep silent.

"You've nearly ninety extra bodies to feed, sir, and only a single pair of hands. You'll excuse us if we'd rather not wait until the end of the day for a single meal. Mistress Tavey sent us to help, and help you we shall. Now," I said, giving the place another glance, "what needs doing?"

The man gaped at me, and Elsie was wide-eyed with astonishment. I felt a blush threatening to burn across my cheeks, but I tipped my chin up and looked the man in the eye, refusing to back down.

A rusty chuckle shook through him, startling me. "Well, now, aren't ye all spit and fire, just like I hear all Irish lasses are."

"Scots Irish, if you please," I corrected. My father wouldn't have wanted me to let that point slide past.

"Oh, Scottish Irish are ye? Well, now, don't that beat all. Fine, then, my fiery miss. Come with me."

He brushed past us. Elsie looked at me. I couldn't very well refuse now. I gave her an encouraging smile that may have looked more like a grimace before following the cook.

He led us down two decks and into a hold stacked with boxes and barrels, with piles of canvas bags filling every available crevice and others hanging from hooks set in the beams.

"The freshest of it all won't last, so we'll have at it first," the man told us, picking through the bags closest to him. "Some fine meals, fer a bit. But later—" He turned to cast a dark-eyed gaze over us. "Later it'll be all salt meat and beans and hard tack. And potatoes and peas."

"Peas?" Elsie looked surprised.

"So it isn't all potatoes, my fine lady" he told her with a grin full of missing teeth, which accounted for his lisp. "There's butter and rum and beer and water, but that last will go sparingly. Captain's careful about the water. We've chickens, aside from those ones ye brought. Biscuits to break yer fast, and peas and butter fer noon, and beans and meat fer suppers, with a measure of beer or rum, depending on the day. There's salt beef and fish, and a thankful thing the fish isn't from that last shipment." Again that gaping grin, this time with a rusty chuckle that shook his narrow body. "Foul lot that was, and Captain fouler still from the trouble it caused."

"What happened?" I asked without thinking.

"Supposing to be salt fish," he answered while hefting bags aside. He was much stronger than he looked. "But weren't all. Had some fresh mutted in. Didn't realize it 'til a two-day from port. Went from Amsterdam to Aberdeen with that stench coming up at us, and then finally pitched the whole of it over the side. Washed the whole place down and still it reeks, but it'll clear in a few weeks yet. Captain was fast fer the devil in his ire, rightly so, and took the whole business to the magistrate. Didn't see any pay of it, but no loss, either, so there's that."

The man was becoming chatty as we lingered. I suspected he didn't have much in the way of company, alone in his galley, and women or not, we'd do for conversation for now.

20

"So these here," he said, gesturing to the bags. "I've fresh beef to go with these cabbages and onions, and fresh bread, too, and eggs and milk. These'll need tending." He pulled out a head of cabbage. "Quartered, thusly." He made a couple of slashing motions. "And the onions the same and the eggs cracked." He patted a small crate. "But fer the noon meal, first, there's butter and bread and a good hard cheese." Lifting the top of another crate, he pulled out a large wheel. "So send them women to me and I'll dole it all out, and then later ye both can have at the cabbage and onions fer the supper."

He eyed us, and I saw a challenge in his gaze.

I nodded. "Of course."

"Fine, then, off with ye. And no women in my galley," he called after us. "I have the charge of it. I won't be sharing the cook fire. I told that woman what came asking already. 'Tis in my trust, and I don't take it lightly."

I held up my hand in supplication. "Of course not, Mr. Beacham. It is your kitchen."

We found our way back to the berths. I wasn't sure whether to laugh or not. Whatever had I been thinking? I was only a few months learning how to cook. How could I possibly do anything but add to Mr. Beacham's work?

"I can't believe you were so bold," Elsie told me. "I'm not ashamed to say he frightened me badly."

"I'm a bit surprised myself," I admitted. I decided not to share my doubts, at least for the moment. "Let's find Tavey and give her the word."

Grahame didn't come below for his luncheon, so I carried it up to him. I found him helping secure one of the sails. It was mesmerizing to watch the men work together, and I was impressed by how seamlessly Grahame had fit in with the crew.

I moved to the rail, not wanting to be in the way, and saw a large cliff, like a flat-topped mountain, jutting out into the lough. It was looming ahead of the ship, like a guardian of a castle entrance.

"That be Magilligan Point." The cook's rough voice came from behind me. He stood a few paces back, carrying a large pail of peas mixed with butter in one hand and a pail of wooden bowls in the other. He had wrapped a discolored length of fabric a couple times around his neck, as though afraid to take chill. The strange scarf hung down his chest in a loop. It had grown chillier out, with a bite in the wind. I wished I'd thought to wear something warmer.

"Ye shouldn't be standing on the rail," he told me. "'Tisn't safe."

"I'll take care not to fall," I said, a bit dismayed that he would think me so careless.

"'Tisn't falling that I'd fear," he said ominously and went on about his

21

duties.

I was staring after him as Grahame approached.

"Did he offer you a wrong word?" Grahame asked darkly.

"No, nothing like that." I shook off the feeling. "I brought your luncheon. The others are eating in the berths."

"Let's sit over here." Grahame led me to a sheltered place near the livestock and accepted the bowl of buttered peas, a wedge of cheese, and hunk of bread. "What do you think of Mr. Beacham?"

His question surprised me, more because he asked it than what he asked.

"The cook? He isn't a pleasant fellow, but he was helpful enough."

"Has everyone settled in?"

"Yes. We're hanging blankets for privacy. I saw Jacky came below."

Grahame merely nodded.

"Will you be working for the whole voyage?" I asked, encouraged by finding him so talkative.

"The captain lost a couple hands in Aberdeen. We've struck a bargain." Grahame didn't say more, and I was uncertain how to press him, so I let it go.

"Will you come below soon?"

"For supper."

That ended my attempts at conversation. I stared toward land as Grahame finished his meal. The coastline was still green and lush, dotted with boulders as if cast about by a giant, like from my nanny's tales.

Watching the shore slide by, I could still believe I would see home again. A long sigh escaped me, and I glanced at Grahame to find him watching me with those dark eyes.

He looked away, then held his bowl out.

"My thanks."

"Of course," I answered, for the lack of any better response.

"I'll see you below."

It was as much of a dismissal as he would give. I gave him as cheerful a smile as I could manage, collected his empty bowl, and returned to the berths.

I fetched my own meal and found Elsie and Jacky lunching near their cots.

Jacky offered me his stool, and I sat, grateful for the company. The rest of the berths was lively with conversation.

"I was just telling Elsie how we'd reach Magilligan Point," Jacky told me. "Once we pass it, it isn't long to round Inishowen Head and be out on open water." He was buzzing with excitement and coming close to hitting his head on the planked ceiling with each gesture.

Elsie was smiling patiently at her husband with a look of amusement and adoration. It was sweet to see, but after the uncomfortable meeting with Grahame, it also reminded me of what was lacking in my own marriage.

"The cook said something strange," I said, trying to shake off my malaise. "He told me that I shouldn't stand close to the rail."

"It would be awful if you were to fall over," Elsie said.

"I thought that was his point," I told her, "but he said that it wasn't falling that worried him. What else might it be?"

I looked to Jacky, but the young man shrugged. "I couldn't say. But I can tell you that sailors are ripe with superstitions. They're worse than spinsters." He laughed.

Jacky returned to the deck to try his hand again at helping Grahame. Elsie and I found where to wash the dishes, though I was still pondering the cook's meaning. The cook had set up a barrel of sea water through the passage leading out of the berths next to my cot. We saw to the dishes, drying them on towels I had brought. I was glad that Grahame had known what to prepare, but as he seemed to have sailed before, I knew I shouldn't be surprised. Some of the others had no dishes at all and had to borrow, or had no suitable dishtowels and shared. Others were dismayed by sharing a single barrel. I hoped it would be emptied each day, at least. And that we wouldn't be expected to bathe with the same water.

I pushed the thoughts out of my head.

Elsie and I returned to the stools by Elsie's cots to work on stitching again. We spoke mainly of needles and knitting, and Elsie was a wealth of knowledge. I knew embroidery, it being the lady's work that my mother most enjoyed, and I knew enough stitchwork to sew a seam or a button. Elsie knew stitches by the score, and she recommended them, shyly at first, and then more emboldened as I readily accepted. I wanted to be better at the work and knew I had a long ways to go. Plus, it did help pass the time.

CHAPTER FOUR

By the time Tavey found us, I was ready to set aside stitchwork for kitchen work, a thought that would never have crossed my mind two months ago.

"Can you two see to helping the cook? We've got others preparing what we've brought for supper, but I'm sure he could use an couple extra pairs of hands."

I readily agreed. Elsie was reluctant but nevertheless joined me. We found Beacham in the galley, muttering to himself. He didn't notice us until I cleared my throat.

"Blast ye, er—" Beacham caught himself quickly and ducked his head. "Beg pardon, miss, thought you were the first mate."

"Does he often come to the galley?" I asked, curious.

"Only by the captain's say. Now, what might I be doing fer ye, miss?"

"We've come to help with the evening meal, as we said we would."

He looked surprised. "I figured ye'd have found better occupation by now than quartering cabbages and onions."

"As it turns out, there seems very little for women to do."

He chuckled, a sinister edge to the sound. "We aren't too much accustomed to women folk aboard, 'tis true indeed. But I'll not say no to help, since ye insisted in it so ably afore. Remember ye where the storage hold be?"

I nodded.

"Then take this," he said, handing me a large cleaver. The handle was smooth with use, and the blade gleamed sharply along its length. "And take ye this," he said, handing a thick, square board to Elsie. "And this." He handed me a bucket. "Fill it and bring it back. We'll do that a handful of times and see where we stand."

I had hoped to ask the cook about his strange warning, but he gave me no chance, turning instead back to his kettle and cutting board.

"Shall we?" I asked Elsie. She looked uncomfortable carrying the board, but she wrangled it into a better hold and nodded.

In the storage hold, we set the board over a barrel and began. Elsie fetched out a cabbage and I had at it with the cleaver. It took me several tries the first few times, and the cabbage was less quartered than hacked into oddly shaped bits. The second one was no better. It didn't help that the ship's movements made the thing roll on the board.

"Try taking a slice off the end first," Elsie suggested.

I did that, setting the cleaver against the cabbage and then sinking my weight onto it. The flatter end helped keep the cabbage from rolling and the work went faster.

We filled the bucket, and I offered to run it up. Elsie was happy to let me face the cook, though she offered to go, too.

"There's no reason for both of us to make the climb," I told her. "I won't be a moment."

The cook was muttering again, and this time I caught a few words. They actually sounded like prayers.

"Excuse me," I called. He faced me, and his expression curled into a sideways grin to see the bucket of cabbage.

"They may not be perfectly quartered," I admitted.

"They'll do, miss," Beacham assured me. He dumped the bucket load into the large kettle.

"If I might ask," I began, then continued when the cook raised his brow encouragingly, "for what were you praying?"

"A smooth sailing," he told me. "Every voyage be different, miss, but each and every one, I pray fer a smooth one."

"Does it work?"

He gave a half-shrug. "Cannot hurt. Once we're past the point, the sea will turn on us. The North Sea is always unhappy this time of the year."

"What does that mean?"

"We'll be tossed about a bit," he said. "Not to fear, mind ye. The captain knows these waters. We'll stay within sight of land fer a day or so, but then we'll be at the mercy of the sea."

I wasn't sure I liked the sound of that.

That evening, the passengers gathered in the hold before supper was served. Mr. Vance led us in worship. I was surprised to find that all of the passengers not only knew each other, they were all of the same congregation. It made sense, I realized, but it only served to make me feel even more the outsider.

At least Grahame had come below to join us. I had never learned how faithful he was, having only sat with him in service before our wedding day. He made all the correct responses, however, and whispered in prayer to himself when the time came. I had to hurry mine, so captivated was I in watching him.

We sat with Jacky and Elsie for this first supper. The stew was passable, though I took more pride in the cabbages than I knew was strictly necessary. The passengers shared other food between them that they had brought, such as apples and bread, meat pies, greens and carrots. It was a hearty meal eaten with laughter and anticipation.

Jacky described passing Magilligan Point, and I realized that was when the cabbages were rolling so badly. We were rounding Inishowen Head now, Jacky told us, and he seemed sorely pressed to be missing it. Elsie took pity on him and sent him upward as soon as he'd finished his meal. He gave his wife a kiss and dashed off.

Grahame thanked both Elsie and I for the meal, touched my shoulder, and followed the younger man to the deck. I stared after him. He'd touched me more in the last day than in the whole of the last month.

Elsie and I returned to the wash barrel and were dismayed to see the same water in the same barrel.

"I'll ask Mr. Beacham about it," I said.

"Oh, I don't want you to get scolded," Elsie told me. "I'm sure it'll sort itself out."

"Nonsense," I said with a lift of my chin.

But then we heard a fuss coming from the berths. We both hurried up the narrow steps to find Iona dressing down Mr. Beacham about the state of the water.

"We won't tolerate the slovenly manners you profess," Iona was saying. She gestured grandly as she spoke. Her back was to us, so I couldn't see her expression, but indignation stiffened her back and punctuated her gestures.

Beacham was staring at the gesticulating woman with narrowed, dangerous-looking eyes, but he didn't move. Nor did he answer. When she wound down, she stood huffing in his path, waiting his response. Beacham said nothing for a long moment, and people in the passage were silent with anticipation.

Suddenly, he tugged his forelock, ducked his head, and I heard his murmured, "Madam." He pushed past her, and she stared after him, stunned. The handful of passengers between him and the passageway moved out of his way as he stomped through, hunched with the weight of the two buckets in his hands. Elsie and I stepped out of the passageway to let him by.

He glanced at me and I saw a twinkle of mischief in his eyes. I also saw the slop he was carrying in each bucket.

"Sir, I say, sir!" Iona's husband was calling after the cook, following him while Iona urged him onward with little taps on his shoulders. Beacham didn't stop but went down the steps toward where the barrel stood on the landing below. I followed Iona as they passed me, and I felt Elsie pressing close behind.

As soon as we reached the landing, we saw Beacham dump a bucket into the water. The slop was brown and nasty and full of bits matter, both vegetable and animal.

Iona gagged. Her husband went silent. The contents of the second bucket followed the first.

Beacham wiped his hands on his trousers, picked up both buckets with one hand, and went back up the stairs. Everyone hurried to make room for him. Silence followed him through the hold until he passed through the other side.

I wanted to cheer for him, and I couldn't say exactly why.

Conversation buzzed around us after Beacham left. I saw a handful of men stomp off toward the exit.

"Why did he do such a thing?" Elsie wondered.

"Maybe to put us in our place," I said. I considered a moment. "It's his ship, after all. We're guests here. We may not like everything that happens on board, but that's no reason to go demanding our own way."

"He let you demand it, though," Elsie said.

She had a point. "Maybe because I was demanding to help."

"What do you think will happen now?"

"I really couldn't say." But I feared the cook would get a talking to from the captain. Or worse.

I stole to the deck as the rest of the passengers made ready for our first night at sea. The sky overhead was quickening into night, but in the brilliant sunset, I could still see land off the rail of the ship. The waves were stronger, though, than they had been in the lough, and to one side of the ship stretched open water. We were sailing past Ireland's northernmost point. By morning, I thought, we will have left home behind.

I swallowed against a rush of emotion. Sorrow and grief, but something more primal, a sense of loss that went deeper than I had the words to describe. I was sailing from my past into an unknown future. I'd felt similarly after my wedding when I'd climbed aboard the wagon that Grahame had brought to take me home with him, but this was more profound. Then, I could have found a way to return to see my parents and the home where I'd been raised and all the other familiar places. How I could do that now, I couldn't begin to imagine.

I felt someone approach and turned to find Grahame joining me. I was several paces off the rail, deciding to take the cook's strange warning to heart. Grahame stood with me, watching Ireland slide by into the gloom of the gathering night.

"I heard of trouble below," he said, speaking low.

"Mr. Beacham and Iona, one of the women," I told him. "Is he in trouble?"

"I suspect so."

"Did you see the men speaking with the captain? Several came up to the deck afterwards."

"I caught the end."

I waited, but Grahame said nothing more. I clenched my fist with frustration.

"And the water barrel?" I asked at last.

"It's dumped each night."

It was something, at least.

"I wonder why he didn't just say so?" I didn't expect Grahame to answer. It surprised me when he did.

"Sailors aren't accustomed to women onboard. They won't take kindly to demands."

"Oh." Beacham had mentioned as much, at least the first part.

"Careful how you speak to them," Grahame warned me, reaching down to take hold of my hand. "Best to avoid them." His hand, large and calloused and strong, threaded into mine.

"I can't avoid the cook," I told him. "We have to make meals and need his help."

"Let one of the others."

I stared up at him, puzzled, but his expression was inscrutable.

"I offered to help him," I said at last.

Grahame looked startled. "Why?"

"Because it needs doing," I answered, startled in return. "And I've the time to spare."

Grahame's expression smoothed into consideration. I watched his jaw work back and forth under his beard before an echo of a smile curved his mouth.

"I need help with the chickens," he told me. "If you have time."

My own smile was sarcastic and it felt good to share this one memory between us. "Well, that is certainly something I've learned to do."

Grahame escorted me below as night closed in around the ship. He held up a blanket without word so I could undress. I got out of my bodice and skirts, hanging them on pegs along with my jumps and pockets. I wrapped in the blanket before Grahame helped me into the upper cot. It swayed alarmingly, and I clung to the canvas edges until Grahame steadied it.

"You'll get used to it," he assured me.

I was still dubious.

"I need to check the animals," he told me. "And finish my duties."

I nodded, drawing another blanket up around me. The chill had followed us below.

He hesitated, then gave me a quick kiss on the forehead before disappearing through the passageway.

I stared after him, stunned.

Eventually, all the lamps but a couple were extinguished, casting the berths into nearly total darkness. I felt the weariness in my very bones. The day had been the longest one I'd lived through since, well, since first going to Grahame's farm. But even still, it took a long while to fall asleep. The cot swayed oddly, the cold seeped in through the canvas, and the sound of ninety others trying to get comfortable enough to fall asleep, and then the snoring that followed, filled the berths for quite a while.

When I finally did drift off, I was plagued by dreams of clinging to the rail as the ship tossed upon the waves while something dark and ominous lurked deep under the roiling surface of the sea, waiting for me to fall.

CHAPTER FIVE

Morning found me unrested and unsettled. The ship lurched and rolled, trying to toss me off my feet once I found a way out of the cot. The lamps had been lit, but the persistent gloom did not help give me any sense of the time. Grahame was already gone and had left his blanket folded neatly in the middle of his cot.

Dressing was an act of athletic ability that I didn't possess. I actually hit my head on the plank wall. I finally sat on my stool to regain a sense of stability. What was going on around us to make the ship move so?

I heard others in the berths moving around and decided to find Jacky and ask him. Or go on deck myself for a look. Gathering myself, I got to my feet, using the walls and the beams to keep upright. The others weren't having any better luck.

I made my way down the berths. Elsie was up and dressed but had planted herself on her own stool, bracing against the wall when she needed support.

"Has Jacky gone up?" I asked her, clinging to the beam.

"Yes." Elsie's voice was pinched. "I asked him not to, but he insisted."

"I'm sure he'll be fine."

"But all this tossing about—what if he's swept overboard?"

"Grahame will watch him," I told her with certainty.

Elsie seemed reassured, if only just.

"I thought I'd go have a look myself," I told her.

"Oh, please don't," Elsie begged me.

"I won't go on deck," I assured her. "I just want to see what is going on outside." And I needed to breathe fresh air.

Elsie was not going to be convinced, but I was insistent. I knew she wouldn't go, so I told her I'd return with news soon. And that I'd take care.

A few of the other passengers had heard me and watched with

trepidation as I made my way through the passage topside.

Outside the skies were grey and ominous with thick clouds. Rain splattered intermittently and the deck was wet. The waves rolled around us, some breaching into whitecaps that sprayed into the air. The sailors were at their work even so, most wearing sturdy coats and a few with hats. I saw Grahame wearing his leather coat, the wide collar turned up against the wind. His head was bare, however, his hair plastered back into its knot. Jacky was nearby, frozen by the middle mast with a look of doubt and fear.

Grahame noticed me and came over to the doorway.

"Stay below," he told me. "See to the chickens."

"I will."

He hesitated, as if he wished to say more but thought better of it. With a final nod, he returned to his work.

I went below, concerned and bracing myself against each swell as I walked. Rather than returning to the berths, I found my way to the galley.

Beacham was in there. He stood with the confidence of a man use to riding waves, swaying with the ship's motion, only catching himself on the deepest lurches. He turned to reach for a ladle and saw me braced in the entrance.

"Goodness me, miss—ye gave me a fright."

"I do apologize."

He waved it away. "It'll be a hot meal to break the fast," he told me. " Porridge and milk and whatever the likes of ye have brought. So I'll not be needing the use of ye now."

"That's fine. I need to take care of the chickens."

"If you see any eggs, ye bring them to me, miss, and we'll see what we can make with them. But I'm doubting you'll find any this day. And mind yer step. They've got the run of their little cranny. Ye know the way?"

"Yes, I think so."

"Ye'll be needing this," he said, and he drew up a lantern from a storage place under his work counter. He lit it from his own, closed the glass, and held it out. "Bring her back when you've finished. I'll have yer meal ready by then."

I took the lantern with gratitude. He nodded and returned to his work.

I found the small room where the chickens had been cooped. It was past the storage hold, and I'd stopped there for a bag of feed. The hold housing the chickens was small and low ceilinged but with a beam for roosting. Straw was piled on the floor around the slatted crates that had carried the chickens to the ship, and the crates were left open for nesting. The place reeked of chicken droppings. I closed the door quickly behind me to keep them cooped, but when I held the lantern out, I realized I needn't have bothered. They were all roosted, clinging tightly to the beam or nesting along the walls in the curve of the outer hull or in the crates. I checked their water and scattered feed for them. Not a one of them stirred.

Concerned, I let myself out again and returned to the galley.

"'Tis the tossing," Beacham told me when I described what I'd seen. "It'll pass." He hoisted two buckets filled with porridge by their rope handles. I hoped they weren't the same buckets from last night, but I was certain that they were. "If ye wouldn't mind, miss, helping me with seeing these to the others?" He asked it with such a strange tone that I wondered once more what the captain had done to him.

It was on my tongue to ask, but he gave me a long look, his eyes glimmering with that dangerous light I'd seen in them before, so I swallowed the words and merely gave him a nod. I picked up the wooden ladle he'd left on the counter.

We passed through the berths, distributing the meal. Beacham said nothing to the others, though he gave Elsie a nod. I noticed the cook getting dark looks, but no one spoke to him, for which I was thankful. He had to return to the galley twice to refill his buckets. When we reached the far end, he set down a bucket to tug his forelock in thanks.

"I'll see to the men now, miss," he told me.

"Shall I help?"

"Goodness me, no, miss. Captain would flay—er, Captain wouldn't like it, you coming topside with this weather. Thank ye, though." He ducked his head towards me and retreated.

I took my breakfast and rejoined Elsie as prayers began.

"I hope it isn't like this the entire voyage," Elsie said after we had eaten.

"I'm sure we'll get used to it," I answered. I noticed that the odor of fish wasn't as noticeable. Either it was passing or I was growing accustomed to it. So I had hopes for the rest.

I told Elsie about the chickens. We shared a laugh, but it was a nervous sound that soon died.

For lack of anything better, I pulled out my knitting. Elsie tried to help me, but between my lack of skill and the ship's motion, I made little progress. Still, it passed the time. Somewhere farther up the berths, a woman began singing. A boy joined in, his voice bright and clear. Others joined in, too, and the song cheered us.

Near lunchtime, I retreated back to my cot to see what provisions Grahame had brought that we could share. I found hazelnuts and apples, dried meat, carrots, leeks, potatoes, and more cabbage. I wasn't sure what to offer, though. Would he want me sharing with the others? Uncertain, I debated going on deck to ask but recalled Beacham's warning about the captain.

The captain hadn't seen me on deck earlier, but Grahame had been quick to send me back below. I doubted he'd be pleased to see me topside again so soon.

I returned to Elsie and found that Jacky had come below and was sitting on his cot. He had changed, though his hair was still wet. His damp clothing was hanging from pegs, dripping water onto the wood planks. Elsie was trying to coax bread into him.

"No, lass, take it away. I've eaten all I can stomach." Jacky looked a bit green and laid back on his cot, a hand over his stomach. Elsie covered him with a wool blanket and looked down at him with concern. I came closer.

"What is it?" I whispered to her.

Elsie shook her head. She pulled a stool over to the head of the cot to sit and reached out to smooth Jacky's hair.

"Shall I sit with you?" I asked, uncertain.

"If you'd like," Elsie answered, but her gaze never left Jacky.

I fetched my own stool and returned. As I did, I heard a few others comment on feeling unwell.

Was it a sickness? The porridge hadn't been that great, but then if it were the food, wouldn't we all be ill? Maybe it was the rough seas, and, like the chickens, we needed to keep still and rest until it passed.

Jacky slept and we took up our knitting again. I remembered my provisions when Beacham came through with a share of butter, more bread, and peas that had been boiled nearly into mush. Jacky refused any of it. I excused myself and trailed after the cook to collect my own share of food.

"Seasick, that's what it is," Beacham told me as he handed over my shares. "Seen it afore. Usually passes after a time. 'Tisn't good it's hitting so early, though," he said with a glance back down the berths.

"Will Jacky get better?"

"Hard to say. Strikes everyone different, it does. Most likely get ye all in the end. 'Cepting yer man, of course. He's seen a ship or two in his day, I'll wager."

I didn't say anything, and Beacham returned to his work. I ate what I could, stowed the rest away, thankful to find a crock to put the butter in, and returned to Elsie and Jacky.

Jacky was still asleep. Elsie was still watching him furtively

"He's never ill," she whispered. "I've seen him soaked to the bone out in the cold and not even a wisp of a fever the next day."

"Mr. Beacham said it's a sea sickness and that it usually passes."

Elsie looked a bit relieved.

Grahame joined us not long afterwards. His hair was wet, but he'd put off his coat. He looked Jacky over, his expression closed. "Did he eat?"

"Only bread," Elsie answered, "when he first came down."

"Get him to drink," Grahame told her. "Not water. Anything but."

Elsie nodded.

I followed Grahame to our cots. "Will he recover?"

Grahame didn't answer. "How are you feeling?"

"A bit unsteady," I admitted. I was regretting the peas and butter for lunch. "Why are we moving like this? Is it the rain?"

"A storm's passing. It makes the seas wild."

"How long will it last?"

"Not long."

I took hope and sat quietly as Grahame ate. I tried to find a subject of conversation but failed. Grahame didn't seem interested in talk. He ate quickly, thanked me, and returned topside.

The seas calmed by afternoon, much to everyone's relief. I checked on Jacky to find him awake and taking bread with beer. Elsie looked relieved.

I returned to the galley and Beacham helped set me up in the storage hold with a cleaver and cabbages.

"I'll be back for them in a bit," he told me. "And mind," he said, pausing at the entrance to the hold, "if the weather turns, ye put down that knife and come up."

"I will."

"And don't go out on deck. Wild seas stir up the deep."

I blinked, but before I could think to ask what he meant, he had gone.

I spent the next hour taking my worry out on heads of cabbage.

By supper time, the motion of the ship had grown even stronger, and Jacky had gotten worse. He'd been sick once when the swells began anew, and now anything he tried to swallow came up again. Several others began to complain of sickness, too, and panic would have struck through the group if the captain hadn't spoken with Mr. Vance and the other men. I tried to listen in but couldn't get close enough. Mr. Vance, however, came through the berths afterwards, asking that we stay calm and rest.

Could it be that simple? I wished it were so easy to cure the sores on my hands. I'd discovered blisters on my palms after handling the cleaver again so soon, and a few had opened. I didn't want to bother Elsie with it, as she had her hands full tending Jacky, and I wasn't sure who else to ask.

Fortunately, I ran into Tavey.

"How are you feeling?" the older woman asked kindly. I knew the question was to see if I was coming down ill, but I choose the opportunity to show Tavey my hand.

"It's a small thing," I lied as the woman tsked over the sores across my palm, "but if you could recommend something?"

"I've just the thing that might help." Tavey took my arm to lead me. We stopped along the berths while Tavey checked on a few of the other passengers before ending up at her cot.

She took out her bag and rummaged through it. "Whatever have you been doing, child?" she asked, glancing over at me.

"Chopping cabbages for the cook."

Tavey paused, her expression one of surprise. "Chopping cabbages gave you those?"

"There were an awful lot of cabbages," I defended, "over the last two days."

Tavey pursed her lips. "Not use to this sort of work, are you?"

I looked down, biting my lip, wondering how to answer. Tavey saved me the need.

"I'd wondered," she said, "when I first met you."

Was it the shawl that had given me away? Or my finer clothing?

Tavey found what she was looking for and straightened. It was a small jar that smelled rich of lemon balm when she opened it.

"It's a salve," Tavey told me. "It won't take much. Rub it on and cover it with a cloth overnight. Do it for the next several nights and you should heal up without taking infection."

I accepted the jar. "Thank you. That's very kind of you."

Tavey gave me a warm smile. "You take care now, lass. Wear gloves if you can. That'll help."

I promised I would try and returned to my own cot. I put the salve on at once, delighting in the smell even though my palms stung from the touch. I found a pair of my gloves, pretty things not made for hard work, and slid one on carefully. Honestly, I told myself, when would I ever wear them again?

I was about to close up my bag when I saw the edge of the shawl. I drew it out, careful to look around first to see if anyone noticed. I ran bare fingers across the linen and over one of the lace flowers. My throat caught at the beauty of it, and how out of place it was.

Had it only been two days since we had left port? And only a month since leaving home?

A month and a lifetime.

I folded the shawl and buried it deep in my bag, along with the memories.

I fixed Grahame's trencher as Beacham passed with the stew. The cook eyed me but said nothing. I took some stew for myself but ate little of it. My stomach clenched at the thought of food.

Grahame joined me after I'd given up trying to eat.

"How are you?" Grahame looked concerned for me, though he'd left me on my own for most of the day.

"Fine," I said, then at his piercing look, added "not completely well, but I'll manage."

"Have you eaten?"

I nodded. I had eaten. Just not very much.

"Good. You need your strength."

"Will it be like this for the entire journey?" I asked, worried.

Grahame looked down the berths where more passengers had taken to their cots early. "It might."

Something in his tone suggested it might even be worse.

The second night was awful. I didn't get sick, thankfully, but others did. The motion of the cot was of no comfort at all, though Tavey had tried to tell us it would be like we were babes again in the cradle. The smell was horrid, sweat mingling with vomit. And the sounds of so many people packed so close together were just as unsettling. There was no hiding from the fact when a passenger became sick. There was no closing out the noise of snoring from those lucky few who could sleep, or the weeping from those who could not. Below me, Grahame was a reassuring presence, but there seemed to be nothing he could do for the others.

The next day it was better. Jacky kept down broth, and a few of the others were eating by suppertime. I was helping Beacham full-time since so many of the other women were either too sick or too busy helping those who were sick to prepare meals. I tried to spend time with Elsie and Jacky, but it wasn't for long. Beacham had endless amounts of work for me, from washing up the trenchers and bowls in seawater to cutting and peeling and scrubbing. How did I wonder what I would do to pass the time?

I would at least know how to put together a stew when it was all over, I thought. Not that it was the best meal, but in a pinch, or at sea, it was useful enough.

I took frequent trips to the deck to breathe in clear air and to see how Grahame was fairing, sneaking out when no one was watching. He worked as hard as the other sailors and seemed content in the work, even under the gray skies. The rain came and went, but the sailors worked on, heedless.

Grahame did seek me out once or twice during the day for meals, and Elsie told me that he came to look in on Jacky as well. It was something to know he was watching out for them.

Mostly, though, I felt helpless and alone. I wasn't a part of the group of passengers like Elsie and Jacky, and I wasn't a part of the ship's crew like Grahame. I had no true place, unless I counted the supply hold.

The fourth day saw heavier rain. The waves lashed the ship. Though Beacham told me this squall was nothing to a true storm, it was enough of one to put those who had weathered the trip so far into their cots, moaning and shivering. By mid-day, I finally took to mine, my stomach roiling with each toss of the ship. My life narrowed into a thin attempt not to vomit, clutching the chamber pot close with my eyes squeezed shut and my teeth clenched. In the end, I lost the battle.

"Ah, miss, ye poor thing, ye just hang on."

I came out of a bout to find Beacham standing at my cot, holding the chamber pot steady for me.

"'Tisn't so bad," he soothed in his rusty voice. "Ye just take deep breaths. Just keep the breaths coming, there's a fine girl. Here's yer man to see ye through it."

Grahame took Beacham's place, taking the chamber pot away to hold a pewter mug to my lips.

"Drink," he urged in a gentle voice.

The liquid smelt of spice, and I drank hesitantly. It was water but mixed with something warm and earthy with a bite to it that erased the traces of vomit as I swallowed. Grahame didn't let me drink too much, pulling the mug away after only a few sips and urging me to lay back.

Time passed in a blur of sleep and sickness. Grahame stayed with me, coaxing bread soaked in broth and sips of the strange water down me. My sleep was haunted by visions of seas boiling over with black bodied creatures with mouths filled with needled teeth and eyes that glowed yellow in the hazy fog. My waking hours were a torment of sickness, my stomach roiling and my body shaking and sweating in turns.

In between, Grahame coaxed more of the spicy drink into me along with broth and bread. Much of it came back up, but not always, until more and more stayed down. My sweating chills subsided. The nightmares retreated.

I woke to find Grahame smoothing my hair back from my face, a gesture my mother used to make when I was ill as a child. It was comforting as nothing else had been, and I fell back asleep, this time into a true sleep, and did not wake again until morning.

CHAPTER SIX

Grahame wasn't there when I woke. I felt weak and sticky, but I managed to swing myself out of my cot. I stumbled upon landing, hanging on to the swinging edge of the cot to keep from falling. The ship spun around me, but after a few moments it settled into its usual rocking motion.

I eased onto Grahame's cot. My head felt light but my limbs were heavy. I was tempted to curl up and let sleep reclaim me. It was unusually quiet in the berths, with only hushed murmurs and the a few moans breaking the muffled creaking of the ship's decks and hull, and the occasional thump from above.

A woman made her way slowly past the berths, stopping to check at every pair of cots. When she drew closer, I realized I recognized her but didn't know her name.

"How are you feeling?" the woman asked. She was older, around Tavey's age, with a careworn look but kind eyes.

"Better," I answered.

"That is good to hear. You rest a bit. You need to get a bit of food in you, quick as you can. I'll send the man with it."

She began to move away, but I raised my hand to stop her.

"How long have I been ill?"

"I couldn't say," the woman admitted.

"Please, can you tell me how Jacky is?"

The woman's face grew shadowed. "Not well, I'm afraid. Elsie seems a wee bit better, but Jacky is weak as a lamb." She gave me a long look. "When you're feeling stronger, maybe you could give us a hand?"

I quickly agreed. I wanted to stand up then and try to make my way to them, but I knew that would be foolish.

Beacham came through carrying a pail of broth that smelt rich of onions. He grinned a gaping smile when he saw me.

"Bless me, but it does me good to see ye roused, miss. Stand a cup of broth, could ye?"

"I think I could, yes." I was surprised to find myself growing hungry from the smell of the broth.

Beacham ladled out a cupful for me and handed me the mug. The scent of broth set my stomach to rumbling.

"Ye sit easy," Beacham told me, "and I'll fetch yer man."

He was off before I could stop him. Rather than call him back, I sipped at the broth. It was cool and watery, but it was a welcome sensation that helped chase the sour taste from my mouth. I sipped slowly, unwilling to force too much upon my stomach for fear of setting the sickness off again, but the broth settled well inside me, coaxing me back towards sleep. I shook it away by swinging my legs over the edge of the cot.

Grahame found me clutching the mug, feet braced by my stockinged toes against the decking to keep the cot from swinging. I was startled by the relief blatant on his face.

He knelt down before me. "How do you feel?"

"Tired," I admitted, "but better."

Beacham hovered nearby, his pail in hand. Grahame took the mug from me and handed it back to the cook. "Is there bread left?"

"No, sir, 'tis gone. But I've been soaking the hardtack and could fetch a bit of that."

"If you will."

Beacham scurried off.

"How long was I sick?" I asked.

"Three days."

I stared at him in disbelief. It didn't seem possible.

"Will you eat?" he asked me.

"Yes. A woman said that Elsie fell ill. And that Jacky was worse."

Grahame's expression tightened. "Everything that can be done will be," he assured me.

"I want to help."

"Of course. When we know you're stronger."

"How long will that be?"

"It takes longer to mend than to fall ill," he said patiently. "You mustn't rush."

"It wouldn't do me harm to sit with them, would it?"

Something in my tone must have carried my worry across to him. He sat back on his heels, considering.

"No, it wouldn't. Eat first, then we'll see."

I didn't push any further.

The hardtack that Beacham brought was a sort of biscuit that had been soaked in broth. It sat in a dough sludge in the bowl, as unappetizing as anything I had eaten before. Still, with both men looking on, I picked up the spoon and forced down a bite. It was tasteless but oddly filling. I took another, which pleased Beacham to no end.

"I'd best be about me duties," the cook said reluctantly. "You take care, miss."

I thanked him, which seemed to please him even more.

Grahame sat with me while I finished the strange meal, watching every bite as though waiting for me to relapse back into sickness. When I finished, he insisted that I lay down. I didn't argue, sleep tugging at me. He pulled the blanket over me and smoothed back my hair with a gentle hand. I wanted to thank him, but I fell asleep before the words would come.

The next two days I spent with Jacky and Elsie, seated on a stool by their cots. The shadows around us were deep, the nimbus of light from the lanterns small and ineffective, as if the flames were afraid to fall ill by touching us. Elsie was improving, taking sips of broth and bites of soaked hardtack, but she had gotten very weak, even more so than I. Jacky, however, refused nearly everything I tried to give him, and when I could coax it down him, it came back up within the hour.

Beacham gave me all the advice he could, from holding Jacky's nose to get him to swallow, which seemed cruel but did actually work a little, to pulping moistened hardtack into a mash to slide into his mouth. I wanted to try water, but Beacham told me it was the worst thing for him.

"Trust me, miss, I seen it afore. Ye try some of that grog afore ye try water, but broth's the best fer him now. The grog won't work when they've gone this long. We got a bit into his little wife, though, and it did her a world of good, just as it did ye."

"You helped her?"

"Me and yer man, sure."

I was profoundly thankful for that, which surprised me. The idea of these two different men helping complete strangers was oddly reassuring. If they could come together to save Jacky, surely he would live.

But though I tried everything Beacham offered, very little of it worked for Jacky. He was pale and feverish under his blanket, and there were times when I worried that his breath had stopped.

Elsie finally came back to herself on the evening of the second night. She was weak and wan, but she offered me a thin smile.

"You're so kind to help us," she murmured, her voice the barest whisper.

I didn't know what to say. I hadn't felt like I was doing much good at all as I watched Jacky grow weaker. But seeing Elsie awake and alert gave me hope.

"Try to drink this," I told her, helping her to sit up a little so that she could sip from the mug. "And then we'll see about something more solid."

"Is Jacky up?" Elsie asked after she'd finished the broth.

I hesitated, and Elsie must have read the worry on me.

"He's not better, is he?"

"No," I answered. "I'm sorry. I've been trying everything I can."

"Help me up."

"Elsie—"

"I need to see him."

I didn't think I was strong enough to help Elsie alone. "Let me fetch help. Please," I added, pleading, when Elsie struggled to move herself. Elsie settled reluctantly.

I hurried as quickly as I could down the berths, looking for someone who might help. More passengers had recovered, but they were all still weak or helping those who hadn't recovered. Beacham was nowhere in sight, and I suspected that Grahame was on deck at his duties.

I finally found Iona standing near the entrance. The older woman looked worn out and carried a hard expression on her face. Still, I approached her.

"Can you help me, please? With Elsie and Jacky?"

Iona's expression tightened. "Not now, girl."

"But Jacky—"

"I said not now." Her voice was hushed but sharp as a knife. I fell into a stunned silence and only then realized I was hearing muffled sobs coming from the berths behind me.

One of the men was cradling a woman close to him, shaking with sorrow. The woman was limp, her arms dangling and her head lolling with each of his shudders. Her skin was pale and her eyes were staring upwards, unseeing.

Dead. The woman was dead.

I stumbled back, horrified. I retreated as quickly as I could, then fled to Elsie. The shadows seemed to reach out as I rushed down the narrow hall, each berth holding horrors within their cots.

I stopped next to the blanket dividing the berths next to Jacky and Elsie. I tried to gather myself, but my heart was hammering and my stomach roiled once more. A cold sweat broke out over me.

People were dying.

I clung to the wood beam as the edges of my vision blackened. I fought against the urge to faint, taking long, deep breaths despite the stench permeating the air. I didn't look at the people in the cots behind me. I was terrified I'd find open, lifeless eyes staring upwards out of slack faces.

Movement from the other side of the curtain finally cut through my panic. Fearful of what I'd find, I stepped around it.

Elsie had worked herself into a sitting position but was leaning heavily back towards the cot. I rushed forward to help support her.

"You need to rest," I told her. My voice was trembling. "Please, Elsie. Please." Crooning the words over and over again, I coaxed Elsie back under the blanket.

"Jacky—" Elsie breathed out his name.

"Just rest," I told her, pleading. "He's here. He's right below you. Please, rest."

When Elsie was settled and her eyelids drooped closed, I busied myself straightening her blanket. I knew I was letting fear take over, but I couldn't help myself. I could not bear to look down at Jacky.

It was Beacham who saved me. He came upon me fussing with Elsie's blanket, tucking it in around her feet.

"He's stopped the shaking, then," Beacham said, his tone sober.

I froze, unwilling to look below.

"'Tis peaceful, this part," he continued. "But let's us keep to trying. Might be we could bring him around yet."

"Do you think so?" I wanted so much to believe him.

Beacham gave me a little shrug. "I seen it once or twice. No harm in the trying, miss."

He offered me a mug of broth and a spoon. I took it and, finally, looked down at Jacky.

He did look peaceful. And still alive.

Pursing my lips, I sat down on the stool next to his cot and began once more to coax dribbles of broth into him.

The next day Elsie was stronger. And insistent. I found that I could help her from the cot unassisted, but she was still frail. I propped her on the stool next to Jacky and stood close at hand, just in case.

"He's still very weak," I whispered to Elsie. "I can't get much down him. Beacham has been all sorts of help."

"I'll get him to eat," Elsie said, weary but determined.

And so for the next few days, I watched Elsie coax, urge, and demand Jacky to eat. At first, he responded to her. He drank more broth. He took small bites of the mushy hardtack. He even opened his eyes and once reached out toward his wife. I went to sleep that night with the first real hope in days.

By morning, however, he was worse. He'd been sick again in the night, so much so that now he refused anything Elsie tried to press on him.

And another person had died in the night, this time one of the children. The wails of grief tore my heart in two, and I couldn't hold back my own sobs.

Elsie still tried to get Jacky to take anything. She was up at all hours, resting only in bits. I took on the task of keeping Elsie strong, seeing that she ate and rested. It was nearly as hard as getting Jacky to eat, but reminding her that she needed to rebuild her own strength to help her husband usually worked.

I wanted to help the others, but I couldn't bring myself to leave the radius of Elsie and Jacky. The others faded to noises and smells, a backdrop of misery that was too great for me to consider. Elsie and Jacky became my entire focus, my world narrowing to the space around their cots, and only when someone came into that small circle did they become real. Grahame came by at least once a day but never for long. Beacham came by more often, carrying his ever-present pail of broth and a face filled with hard-edged sorrow. Tavey came by once, herself weak and wan, and she did not linger. She offered Elsie a few encouraging words that none of us believed before continuing down the berths.

At the end of the second week of our voyage, Jacky died.

I was sitting on my stool by the wooden beam, watching Elsie in prayer. I wanted to pray with her, but I was so tired that I couldn't form the words.

"Jacky?" Elsie said her husband's name with a tinge of panic.

I stood, fear taking hold of me. Elsie was shaking Jacky, trying to get a response from him.

"Jacky? Can you hear me? Won't you wake, just for a moment?"

His head lolled, and I pulled back in horror. Elsie's cry filled the air around them.

"Jacky!"

Others came into the space, pressing around Elsie and the cot. I let myself be pushed farther from her side as Mr. Vance, Tavey, Iona, and a handful of others came together. Elsie's cry turned to a sob, stabbing me with grief.

I fled.

I hated myself for doing so, but I couldn't face it. It was too big for me, the pressing grief, the horror, the hopelessness. I fled, finding myself halted in the supply hold. I fell upon the hard, uncaring planks and sobbed.

I didn't know how long I knelt there, sorrow and fear tearing at me, before large, gentle hands urged me to rise. I let myself be raised from the deck and found myself folded into Grahame's embrace. He held me, and I clutched him as sobs racked my body. He weathered the worst of it until I was too exhausted to continue. Then he picked up me and carried me out of the hold.

The fear of returning to the berths where death lay in wait made me fight against him, but he hushed me and kept going past the entrance to the berths. He didn't stop until we were out on the deck of the ship.

The sky was a brilliant blue, like nothing I had ever seen. The wind was cold and crisp and chased the stench of sickness away from me. Surrounding the ship was nothing but water, an ocean of blue-green like I had never imagined. Waves lulled around us, swells like gentle ripples in supple cloth. The sails snapped overhead and the beams and ropes creaked with the strain of the wind.

It was like coming out of hell and into paradise. How could two such different places exist on one vessel? Below was death and sickness and darkness, but on deck was sunshine and wind and the occasional bluster of male laughter.

Grahame set me down upon the deck near the rail. He released me, but he stayed close by. The wind carried a damp spray with it, just enough to feel the moisture from the sea, to taste the salt, so similar to my own tears. The peacefulness soothed my battered soul, cleansed my tired and aching body, and, surprisingly, let loose an anger I had never felt before.

"Jacky is dead," I said, my voice barely loud enough to be heard. "Jacky is dead," I said again, putting force behind the words. I wanted the world to know it.

"I know," Grahame answered, solemn.

I looked up at my husband, a man I barely knew. Elsie knew Jacky, knew him like long-time friends and lovers should know one another. Knew him and had lost him and now would face a strange new land alone.

I had a husband I didn't know and would also face a strange new land alone.

"Why?" I demanded. "Why are we doing this? What was so wrong with Donegal? With your home? With our country? Is all this worth it? All this death and illness and hardship?"

Grahame stared at me, silent, his dark eyes unreadable.

"Why are we doing this?"

When Grahame still didn't answer, I fought the urge to slap him. Anything to get a response from him.

"Why me?" The whine in my voice was unmistakable.

Grahame's lips parted, as though he might answer, but then closed again. He looked away, out over the ocean, the wind tugging at his hair. He struck me as such a sober, solitary person, much like he had when I first met him. Why would such a man want a wife like me? Why would he want a woman like me for a voyage like this? Of course, any man would have wanted my dowry, but to claim it and still take me on a voyage like this? It made no sense. None of it made any sense.

"Will you please talk to me?" I pleaded.

He bowed his head. "I'm sorry for Jacky," he said at last.

I blinked against a quickening of tears, waiting for more.

Grahame turned away.

I stared at him, watching as he walked down the length of the ship. I felt hollow inside and bruised and battered on the outside. And alone. So alone.

What must Elsie be feeling?

Guilt filled the hollow place inside of me. Without another glance for my husband, I left the deck, returning to the berths and the hell they held to seek out Elsie and offer her whatever comfort I could.

CHAPTER SEVEN

I didn't understand how they would hold a funeral on the ship, but as they had already held four, there must be a way. I'd missed the others, busy as I'd been with Elsie and Jacky, but the reminders of loss were ever-present.

Mrs. Wurthing, the mother of the child who had died, still sobbed late into the night, and I found that I missed the fair-haired boy running up and down the passage with his fellows, his laughter light and inviting everyone to join in. He'd had such a lovely voice, too, when he sang with his mother.

Clancy O'Leagh wandered the berths in a daze since his wife's death. I thought of Mrs. O'Leagh often, unable to shake the image of those sightless eyes. I wished I'd known the woman when she had been alive and could bring up other memories of her. Mrs. O'Leagh haunted my nights, though, as an unshakeable presence of staring eyes and slack features in the background of even pleasant dreams.

Mr. Finn had no family aboard to mourn his passing, but plenty of the passengers had called him friend and spoke of his generosity and faithfulness. Mr. Bell, however, was unchanged after his wife's death. I heard Tavey tell Iona that it had been the third wife he'd buried.

But how does one bury at sea? I had never found the nerve to ask. Today I'd see for myself.

The morning after Jacky's death, I gathered with the rest of the men and women who were able to walk to the top deck. Elsie and I walked arm in arm, as much for comfort as for support, following Mr. Vance and Tavey. Mr. Vance recited passages from his Book of Common Prayer as we walked. Elsie moved in a fog, her face pale and her eyes unfocused. She had sat up all night with Jacky's corpse in silent prayer. I murmured the responses, too focused on Elsie to pay heed to Mr. Vance's recitations. I'd have sat up, too, except Tavey had called me away.

46

"Give her the last hours alone," she'd urged me gently. I had retreated to my own cot, but I hadn't slept.

On deck, the air was cold. The sun was still low in the east, risen just above the water, and the sky was streaked with banners of clouds whose undersides shone gold above the blue-green waters. The wind didn't blow as briskly and the sails sagged, as though bowing in respect for the man who had been so keen to know their ways.

Jacky's body lay swathed in sail cloth on two stacks of crates near the rail of the ship. The mourners gathered near, and Mr. Vance came forward, solemn and sorrowful, to read from his book.

"Man that is born of a woman is of few days and is full of trouble. He cometh forth like a flower and is cut down. He fleeth also as a shadow and continueth not . . . ."

Elsie clutched my hands. All I could think was how Jacky would never see flowers again, or a shadow, or another morning like this, so bright and full of hope. Trouble or not, how much better would it have been to live? I knew I would never voice such thoughts, but I couldn't stop them from swarming in my mind. They circled around and around in an endless spiral of sorrow until tears were streaking down my face.

When the singing began, I forced myself to focus on the words, searching for a bit of solace, but the only comfort I had was Elsie's nearness.

Mr. Vance closed his book at last and stepped aside. I looked at Elsie and found her dry-eyed and calm, almost beatific in the way she was staring out toward the sea. I wondered what she had heard in the words to give her such repose.

Elsie released my hands and stepped forward. She placed her hands over where Jacky's own were folded under the sail cloth. She lowered her head, but she didn't speak or sob. She stood there, quietly, with only the sound of the waves and the wind and the creaking ship filling the air. And then she stepped back. I took her hand, heedless of the tears rolling down my cheeks.

The captain stepped forward. He gestured and three sailors stepped up to the crates. One of the men was Grahame. The three took hold of Jacky's shrouded body, and as Mr. Vance said a few last parting words, they cast Jacky over the side of the ship.

I was stunned with horror. I might have cried out if Elsie hadn't sagged next to me. Instead, I caught her as others came forward to help. Together we guided Elsie back to the berths and the darkness that awaited us.

Elsie had finally fallen asleep. I had helped tuck her into Jacky's cot and sat with her. Tavey came by often, giving me a sad smile as she paused to check on Elsie, and then she'd be off once more. Beacham came by as well, offering a mug of something hot to drink. I tried to coax a bit of it into Elsie when she woke, but she turned her head without word. The drink was bitter, but not unpleasant, and warmed me until I, too, felt my head nodding toward sleep.

Quiet voices drifted through the berths, lulling me deeper, until I started out of rest.

"It's the child I'd be afraid for." It was Iona, who didn't seem to know how to whisper. Her voice carried full and clear down the berths. "Coming into the world in a new land with no father. What will Elsie do?"

"She'll manage," Tavey answered. "Just as we all would."

I watched her sleeping. Elsie with child. Of course, I remembered now. Tavey had mentioned a couple of women were carrying when I'd first met the group on the docks, but I had never thought to ask who. And now, with horrible realization, I understood the depths of Elsie's grief. She hadn't merely lost her husband, she'd lost the father of her unborn child.

What would she do? I couldn't bear to think on it. It was tragic and heart-breaking and how would Elsie face it?

Determination stirred inside of me. This was my friend. I would do what I could to help. Elsie didn't have to face it alone.

"You're a quiet one," Beacham observed.

I was sitting in the passage outside the galley door, peeling the bad spots off potatoes. Beacham had the fires lit to cook what would pass as our supper—potatoes and salt beef with dried peas brought up with a bit of water. He'd put me outside the galley so that he could put the potatoes in the kettle as soon as I'd finished with them. "To keep them from browning," he'd told me, but given how they looked when he brought them out, I didn't see what the difference would be.

I didn't feel much like talking. There was constant noise in the berths, and the silence was a welcome respite. It was one of the reasons I kept coming back to help Beacham.

"Shouldn't you be with your friend?" he asked, not unkindly.

"She's resting."

Elsie wasn't resting. She lay in her cot, staring at the wall without seeing. Tavey said it was grief and shock and that it would pass. It had been over a week, though, since Jacky's death, and I was beginning to doubt she'd ever come out of it. I managed to coax food and drink into her, and once got her to wash and change from her stained clothing, but little else.

I sat on a hard stool with a large wooden bowl perched on my lap filling with peels. To one side of me stood a bag of potatoes, on the other a bucket filling far too slowly with those I'd peeled. I was beginning to think that I would be better at knitting than peeling. I'd nicked my thumb several times and had a strip of cloth wound around it.

"Most everyone's back on the mend," Beacham said, breaking the silence with his rusty voice. "The captain's pleased."

"Is he?" I said it to make noise, not really caring what the captain thought. He was a figurehead, like a lord in a tower or a distant king. I only saw him rarely and had never spoken with him. I'd never even learned his name.

"Oh, surely. It pains him to see folks ill. And to lose one—"

"Five," I interrupted, a catch in my voice. "We've lost five."

"I know it, miss."

Silence pervaded. I found I didn't like the silence so much after all. It left me too much alone with my thoughts, which always seemed dark.

"You never did say why I shouldn't stand at the rail on deck," I told Beacham. "And I saw a few of the other sailors keep away. Why is that? Is it because you fear falling overboard?"

"In a gale there's that fear," Beacham said, turning away from the kettle to look down at me. He was still an unsavory looking fellow, with stained clothes and lank hair and a glimmer to his eyes that wasn't entirely welcoming, but there was intelligence there, too, and a measure of care in the lines of his face. I couldn't begin to guess his age. "But there are other fears, too."

"Such as?"

He sniffed. "You don't want to be hearing no sailor's tales, miss. You'd never sleep at night."

"I already don't sleep at night."

He eyed me, as though trying to read the heart of me. He set aside his ladle and hooked a stool with his leg, pulling it out to sit down in the galley entrance.

"There's places in this world, miss, what are still wild. Wild in ways the likes you've never seen."

"Ireland can be wild—"

"Oh, and England, too, in places," he interrupted me. "But not like this. In a place what has never seen the touch of man, there be creatures what'll open a body from—" He stopped himself. "Well, they be deadly, these creatures."

"Have you seen one?"

He looked down for a moment. "Not with me own eyes, no. But I've spoken to those what have. I recall a fellow, German he was—we met in a pub in Calais. He had a tale, he did, of something in the water what rose where they lay anchored off the port of Tunis. Grabbed a man right off the ship, it did, and dove back into the sea, taking the poor blighter with it."

"Grabbed him?"

"That it did. The German saw it happen."

"What did it look like?"

"He couldn't really describe it. T'were dark, he said," Beacham defended. "Said it were man height with arms of a sort, but it had no head, or at least no neck, as I understood him. Head and body all were of a one."

"Did it have legs?" I was curiously fascinated by the tale.

"He didn't think so."

"How did it stand?"

"Gracious, miss, you should be a magistrate with all them questions."

I blushed lightly, but I still pressed him. "Have you ever heard of anything else like it?"

"Not like that, no, but I know other tales. The German, he was right full of them. Said where he came from, the woods still howled with wolves what would eat the children. And then there was a fellow from Venice what spoke of some things coming into the house from the canals."

"Canals?"

"Venice be full of them. Waterways running all through the city. They use them like roads, with boats instead of wagons."

I grinned. "Now I know you are jesting."

"On my honor, miss." Beacham covered his heart with his hand. "And by the grace of God, I swear it be true."

"You've been there?"

"No, but I knew a man what had."

I laughed, not harshly, but with the first real pleasure I'd felt in weeks. "What else did the German tell you?"

"Of flying fish and dolphins what saved a man and a whale eating an octopus."

I laughed, and Beacham chuckled his rusty laughter with me. He sobered then, standing, and reached for the odd scarf he wore when on deck that he otherwise kept hanging just inside the galley entrance.

"He gave me this, though, the German did." He held the scarf out. "Said it would keep me safe."

"Does it?"

"I'm still here, ain't I?"

I took the scarf. It was all of one piece, the ends connected to make a large circle, and made of raw wool that once was white but had turned dingy with wearing. The knitting was finely done, made from better skill than I possessed. No, not knitted. I pulled at it, stretching the stitches to see how they were done, but they made no sense.

"I've never seen it's like," I admitted.

"His mother made it for him, the German told me, when he went from home. All the men of his village wear them when they travel, he said, to protect from the wolves."

"How?"

"Maybe it keeps them off their neck," Beacham said. He took the scarf back. "I couldn't say. All I know is that he swore by it and gave me this one."

"That was kind of him."

"He had it extra, from a friend what had died. And since he couldn't pay fer his beer, I offered to," Beacham said, his eyes narrowing shrewdly, "if he give me the scarf. So it were a trade of sorts."

I understood at once. I could picture Beacham listening to the frightening stories the German sailor told, growing more and more pale, and seeing his chance for a source of protection. After hearing only a few stories, I wished I had such a scarf, too, or the skills to make one.

"Well, I shall stay off the rail," I assured him. "Unless I am wearing one of those scarfs."

"You do that, miss." Beacham looked relieved.

When I returned to Elsie's side, I found her still awake and still staring.

"Beacham just told me the most marvelous tales," I whispered to her. I pulled out my stool to sit next to the cot and began repeating the story to Elsie about the scarf. I didn't talk about the man being pulled overboard— it was too reminiscent of Jacky's loss—but I embellished the tale of Beacham at the pub in Calais with the German sailor, making a tale out of it like my nanny used to do when I wouldn't settle for sleep. She would tell tales of giants and the fair folk and St. Patrick driving out the snakes.

"And so that is why he wears that awful scarf," I finished. "He thinks it will keep him safe."

"Does it?" Elsie's voice was weak and far away, but it was the first she had spoken in days.

"He says he's still alive, so it must."

Elsie sat up, stiff and slow, to face me. "Do you think something like that would have helped Jacky?"

I bit my lip, uncertain how to respond.

Elsie let out a long breath. "No, no, I suppose not. If prayer and broth and everything we tried didn't, how would a scarf?"

"Elsie—"

But Elsie laid back down and turned over toward the wall.

I looked down at her, uncertain what to do, and decided to let her rest. I pulled my bag over and took out my knitting. I had worked on it, a few rows at a time, as I sat with Elsie, but never for long. It looked awful.

I tried to loop the yarn a different way, to see if I could make it look like Beacham's scarf, but the loops merely fell off or came apart. Of course I'd not be able to recreate it. I couldn't even finish a simple shawl. But something in the way Beacham spoke of the scarf had me wanting to try. I knew it wouldn't have saved Jacky, but it held some power over Beacham.

51

Or held power for him, like a relic or a blessing. Foolish thoughts, I knew, but then given all we had suffered, what could it hurt?

Besides, it was different work to try and kept my hands and my mind busy, so that I didn't dwell on death and discomfort and my hurting thumb.

CHAPTER EIGHT

After a harrowing first few weeks, we all improved in health if not completely in spirit, and life on the ship settled into a routine. While I never came to feel completely accepted by the others, I at least had found a place onboard helping Beacham and spending as much time as I could with Elsie. I was able to coax Elsie to sit with me outside the galley while I peeled potatoes or chopped onions or salt beef while we listened to Beacham tell stories he had gathered during his travels. We learned that the *Resolution* was the third ship he had served aboard, that he had started out as a deck hand, repairing and keeping the ship's tackle in good order. He'd been to nearly every port in Europe, many along the Mediterranean, and had been to the New World once when the *Resolution* had traveled to the West Indies. He had stories ranging from pirates and ghost ships to storms and shipwrecks to strange customs in far off lands.

I was transfixed by his tales. I didn't know how Elsie felt about them, for she spent most of the time silent and withdrawn, but I was captivated. The stories drew me out of my own fears and worries, giving me something other to think about than my discomforts and the uncertainty of the future. They reminded me of my nanny's tales, usually dark and deadly stories, and often with a purpose—be it as simple as 'keep off the rail.' That advice seemed to serve Beacham on numerous occasions, from storms to pirates to walking the docks at night.

Though I asked to see it several times, I had no luck knitting anything that resembled Beacham's strange German scarf. I kept at it, as it was more enjoyable than muddling along on a shawl I knew would turn out horribly. It became a quest of sorts to try to master it.

The days got colder and the nights bitter as we traveled. I saw Grahame only once or twice a day, and while I exchanged a civil word with him, I was beginning to realize that instead of bringing us closer together, this voyage had drawn us apart. We spoke little during the brief times we spent together, and though I could see the hint of deep thoughts within his gaze, he never voiced them. He was even more reserved than before, offish and aloof.

Back in Ireland, we spent our evenings alone together, quietly finishing the day's work. While the quiet had been awkward, I knew it had stemmed from the newness of our relationship. I had hoped it would pass with time

On the ship, I felt suspended in a purgatory of doubt. Grahame was my husband, but now it was only in name. He was courteous but distant, keeping to the decks or to other duties and leaving me to my own keeping. I watched the other men among the passengers, and most of them stayed below decks with their families, helping topside only when the need arose. Grahame's bargain with the captain seemed to be one he alone had made, and he was using it to keep away from me. I couldn't imagine what I had done to earn this distance. Was he having doubts of our marriage? Did he regret it? The thought plagued me, but I had no way to relieve my anxiety when Grahame was only around long enough to bid me a good day.

On a clear but cold afternoon, I coaxed Elsie to the deck to walk in the fresh air. We wore several layers of clothing and had wrapped in blankets to help ward off the chill. We walked on the forecastle deck to stay out of the way of the work below. I had no better idea of how the sailors worked the ship than I had when we first boarded, but they were always busy at some task. I often came on deck for the fresh air and watched them at their work. Inevitably, my gaze would seek out Grahame.

"There's Grahame," Elsie said. I had already found him seated amongst a few other sailors, working with rope. The other sailors were talking, laughing at one another, but Grahame sat quietly, mindful of his work.

"He was very kind to help us," Elsie said. "Like you were."

I gave her a sad smile.

"He is of a sober turn, isn't he?" Elsie continued. She hadn't spoken much since Jacky's death, so it was good to hear, but I wasn't sure I wanted to speak of Grahame when my thoughts were so tossed about on the subject of him.

"Yes, he seems so," I answered cautiously.

Elsie glanced at me. "Did you not know him well before you wed?"

"I didn't know him at all."

Elsie didn't look as though she knew what to say to that. "I didn't mean to pry."

"No, you aren't." I turned away to walk towards the prow of the ship. The wind tugged at my cap and pulled tendrils of hair free to whip across my face. The cold numbed my nose and cheeks, but the air felt fresh, and I drew in deep breaths of it.

"Is he kind to you?" Elsie asked.

"In his way, I suppose." I tugged my blanket tighter around my shoulders. "He is still such a stranger."

"How did you meet?"

"Through my father." I studied Elsie. "You don't want to hear all this, do you?"

"It helps," Elsie answered. "It takes my mind off of things."

"Beacham's stories do that for me."

"His stories are too dark for my tastes. I want to hear something of life. Real life, not a sailor's tale. But if you'd rather not—"

"No, it's fine. I've not spoken of it, that's all." I glanced around, noting how close we were to others. The sailors nearby were at their work and not paying us any attention.

"My father met him first during a trip to Lifford. They did business together, or did business with someone they both knew, I'm not clear on that. They got to talking, though, and made a sort of arrangement for Grahame to bring a herd of sheep to my father to sell. Father does all sorts of business," I added. "Running tenant farms and bartering livestock and goods and the like. When Grahame came, I guess he took a liking to me and asked about marriage. That was about three months ago."

"Did he not court you first?"

"He lived a fair distance," I told her. "He was kind enough, and he brought me a couple gifts. A silver comb and a necklace and a ring. They were all very fine," I added, then regretted it. Elsie didn't seem the sort to care about worldly goods.

"Was it a fine wedding?" Elsie sounded a bit wistful.

"I don't know about that. We went to Letterkenny, to the church there, for the ceremony. Mostly family attended. Grahame had a neighbor stand up for him, he and his wife and daughter. The daughter was kind. She helped me that first month."

And I still can't remember her name, I thought. Just the look of her, all elbows and chin and the strange way of laughing she had. But she had been kind, I realized, not mocking as I'd first thought. But then, I'd expected to be mocked or cut or disregarded completely. That had become my social life. It had been refreshing to have even a poor farmer's daughter offer me attention. I shook my head, ashamed with myself.

Elsie was watching me, as if she knew that I was holding back important pieces of the story.

"Why did you decide to leave Donegal?" she asked at last.

"Grahame had already decided it before we wed. He'd been making plans for the last year, or so I understand. He has a brother," I added, "at the colonies already. We're to meet him. There might be other family, too, I think, but I'm not sure on that."

Elsie gave me a thin smile. "You're not too sure on a lot of things to be making such a long journey."

I blushed. "I know." My voice was small.

Elsie paled. "Forgive me, Ailee, that was cruel. I didn't mean to sound so harsh."

"It's nothing but the truth," I told her. "And I know it."

"You didn't ask him about leaving?"

"I didn't know about it until a week before we made the trip to Londonderry. Oh, I see it now, when I think back on it. Selling off livestock and goods, and the visits from the farm's owner. But I've never lived on a farm, so I didn't know that wasn't usual. And then I was so . . ." Shocked? Surprised? Scared? I didn't have a word for the emotions that had overwhelmed me when Grahame had finally shared his plans.

"That wasn't fair of him," Elsie said, looking darkly towards where Grahame sat with the other sailors. "He should have made it clear from the beginning."

"He did, to my father at least," I said quickly. "I just didn't understand."

"He should have made sure you did. Did you even want to come? You could have stayed and married another—" Elsie stopped talking. I had blanched and turned away to try to hide my reaction.

"Ailee, is there something else?"

"No, it's fine. I would have come regardless. Truly." I tried to smile, but I could feel how sickly it must look. I wanted to blurt it all out then and there, all the mistakes and hopes and dashed dreams and the disgrace that followed.

"There is something you aren't saying," Elsie said unexpectedly.

I hesitated, trying to think of anything to say to dissuade her and failing.

Elsie's gaze softened. She took my hand. "I'm your friend," she told me quietly. "Please know you can tell me anything and it won't change what I feel for you."

A wrench of pain had me suck in my breath. "You don't know what it is," I managed to say. I didn't know what I would do if I lost Elsie's friendship.

"Did someone die from your carelessness?"

"What?" I was taken aback. "No. No, of course not."

"Was another life ruined?"

"No, well, not another's."

"Then," Elsie said solemnly, "you have nothing to fear. You cannot possibly lose my friendship for anything less than those."

I hesitated again, and Elsie put her arm around my shoulders. "You can tell me anything," she said gently. "I already know something has happened to you, something you fear to speak of. I don't want you to be afraid to speak to me. I'll respect your wishes if it is too difficult to put into words, but I need you to know that I'll be free to imagine the very worst. So if you can speak of it, please do."

It was a masterful bit of logic. I had to admire Elsie's skills. They rivaled my mother's when it came to ferreting out secrets. Only Elsie did so kindly, offering a way out but adding just a touch of guilt. It wasn't a threat but the honest truth, and I appreciated honesty, more now than ever.

I drew a deep breath. Elsie must have realized she'd convinced me, because she embraced me tighter for a moment in encouragement.

"At the harvest dance, I had several turns," I began. "I usually did. There wasn't a man I fancied yet, though a couple had come courting in the last year. That night, though, I danced with a man who was new to town. He and his wife had moved from Dublin that spring. I had seen Mrs. Kerk around, of course, and my mother had her for tea not long after, but she wasn't a very pleasant woman. Hard," I said, trying to explain. "Iona reminds me of her a little, but without the moments of kindness."

Elsie nodded that she understood.

"That night at the dance, Mrs. Kerk wasn't there. She'd gone visiting family, I was told."

"Told by who?"

My cheeks reddened. "Her husband. He asked me to dance. He was a gentleman about it. He was such a gentleman." I sighed, then stopped myself. "Wallace was his name. Wallace Kerk. He didn't flirt or try to move me, like the other men did. He simply spoke with me like I was worth speaking to, not just being seen with. It was nice."

It had been more than nice. It had been eye-opening. I couldn't recall a time before when anyone had treated me as more than a pretty face or a dowry to be won.

"I saw him at the market the next week and we walked together. He was funny," I said with a smile. "He could make me laugh."

I paused, trapped in the memory of his laughter and how his cheeks wrinkled and his eyes lit up. How he seemed only to see me.

"You fell in love," Elsie said quietly.

I bit my lip and nodded.

"How did your parents find out?"

Elsie had a remarkable grasp of the situation. I was glad for it. I wasn't sure I could relive it all while trying to explain and not fall apart on the deck. As it were, I was glad Grahame had moved out of sight.

"Mother saw us out together one day. We'd met on the edge of town and he'd taken me driving in his carriage. He had a fine carriage," I added, but then I felt silly. "That's a ridiculous reason to go out with a married man, but none of the men who courted me kept a carriage."

"It was exciting," Elsie guessed.

"Yes, it was. But we drove too close to town and Mother saw us. I didn't know she'd gone out to visit Mrs. Dunnelly. I didn't see her, though, so when I got home, I pretended that I'd been out at tea with friends. It was awful," I said, recalling the way Mother had turned on me, the betrayal and outrage on her face, the hushed way she spoke, as though not wanting to be overheard talking to a ruined girl.

"Did you—" Even Elsie couldn't bring herself to voice the question. Mother had sounded the same.

I responded the same way I had to Mother, with a single, devastating nod.

Elsie took a long breath. "He was no gentleman."

"I know."

Silence fell over us. I longed for Elsie to speak but feared what she might say.

"How did you meet Grahame?" Elsie's question was once more unexpected, and her tone was curious without a hint of judgment or reserve. I breathed a sigh of relief.

"He did come to do business with Father. By then, rumors had gotten around. Father and Mother were desperate to make a match for me, and Father increased my dowry. A few men were willing, but they were . . ." I struggled to find the right word. They had been older, widowed men or reckless, indebted men. No one I would have chosen in normal circumstances. I had known my father was going to make a match for me soon. He had no choice if he hoped to salvage any reputation for my younger brothers. But I couldn't face a life with a man such as would want me then.

"Not right?" Elsie completed the sentence delicately.

I nodded. "Not that I should have argued," I admitted, "but they were all so . . . not right." There had been a horrible row with Mother about it, and we had said hurtful words to each other that I knew we'd never be able to forget, even though we'd forgiven.

"I don't think Father even considered Grahame a possibility," I continued. "I'm not even sure how Grahame found out about me. Father didn't say anything, I know, in case the rumors had gotten to Grahame that might spoil the deal. Father had plans to sell the sheep herd in the north where the rot had been so bad. Father was always looking to make deals like that."

Like the one he hoped to make for me, I thought.

"When they met to finish the deal, Grahame asked after me. Father arranged for him to meet me. And that was that, really." I tried to play it off, but Elsie gave me a long, steady look that told me she wasn't buying it.

"Well, not entirely," I admitted. "Mother was opposed to it. She wanted me married to someone in town, not to a . . ." I couldn't find a delicate way to put it.

"A common farmer?" Elsie supplied knowingly.

I nodded, a bit ashamed. I'd shared Mother's feelings about the common part, but I hadn't wanted to remain in town.

"I couldn't stay. I knew the rumors would continue to follow me. I saw a way out of them. And Grahame was kind. I told Father to make the arrangements, but only if Grahame knew the truth. I didn't want to go into a marriage with a falsehood hanging between us."

"You made the decision?" Elsie looked surprised.

"I admit I didn't know what I was getting into," I told her with a wan smile. "I had no true idea how much work it was, being wed to a farmer. But I knew I had to leave town. I couldn't live under such a shadow, no matter that I'd earned it. And he's . . . handsome," I added with a blush.

"He is that," Elsie agreed.

We exchanged looks and then we both laughed. It felt good to laugh. It felt freeing. I had shared the worst thing about myself, and Elsie accepted me anyway. I'd never known a friendship like this before. I couldn't imagine it ever ending.

CHAPTER NINE

"Grahame—" I hesitated, uncertain he'd heard me. There was still time to back away, leave him to his work, talk to Tavey or Mr. Vance instead.

No, he was my husband. I should be able to take my concerns to him.

He had heard me. He stopped on the stairs, turning to face me, his expression guarded.

I mounted the steps to come close enough to talk low.

"I've been thinking about Elsie," I began, "and what she'll do now without Jacky. And—"

"I've spoken to Vance," Grahame interrupted. "Family is waiting for her. A cousin."

I remembered then that Elsie had spoken of letters from a cousin. "Of course. And he'll be there for her?"

Grahame stepped down, his gaze boring into mine. I didn't back away, though I wanted to, and I didn't look away, though it was with an effort.

"She's your friend and you're worried, but Vance will see she's safe."

I wasn't completely satisfied with that.

Grahame laid his hand on my shoulder, and the weight was foreign and startling, but not unwelcomed. An urge to curl up against him made me lean forward, but I stopped myself.

He turned away to continue up the stairs, taking his hand off my shoulder and leaving a hollow chill where the warmth had been.

That was it, then, I realized. I hadn't gotten the chance to plead for Elsie to come with us. Grahame had already worked it out with Vance.

It meant something that Grahame had looked into the matter, though. It showed a kindness in him, or at least a care for me or for Elsie.

Why was it so easy to see a rough, unapproachable side to him? He'd done nothing against me. He was quiet, yes, and kept his thoughts to himself, but he'd taken care of me when I was sick, and he'd helped Jacky and Elsie, too. He'd never offered a harsh word or hand to me. He'd even been gentle.

And he'd dragged me across the ocean away from my family and everything I'd ever known without so much as an apology or explanation. He'd looked into Elsie's future, but he wouldn't help her. He spent as much time away from me and the others as he could.

I sighed. He was a puzzle, and I still wasn't certain where I stood with him. I wondered if I ever would.

I chose this, I reminded myself. Not this exactly, I thought, but I'd chosen Grahame and all that came with him. Even if that included a new world. And if I wanted things to be different between us, maybe I needed to be the one to change them.

Determined, I followed after my husband.

The morning was bright and clear, as fine a day as any I'd hoped to see. The sea was blue, the wind cold, but the sunlight felt good on my face. I looked for Grahame but didn't see him from my place by the passageway. I eased out and worked towards the rail, only to see the captain turning my direction.

Quickly, I hurried to the lee of the quarter deck where the captain wouldn't spy me. There was still no sign of Grahame. The rail was close, but not quite within reach. I followed the wall of the quarter deck to the stern of the ship.

"It's the natives I'd fear," I heard a gruff, thickly accented voice saying. I froze. The voice came from around the corner of the quarter deck where the deck thinned to a narrow passage between the deck and the rail of the ship. "I've not forgot those tales of Roanoke."

"'Tis a hunnert and fifty years past," another voice admonished. "We've towns now, and men. Men with guns. I fear no native."

"I'd fear no man," a third voice said, speaking low in an ominous tone.

"Not that again, Rakes," the first scoffed.

"Yer gettin' to be as bad as Beacham," the second said.

"You mark me," Rakes told them. "If you leave the ship when we make port, you'll stay to the town and to the lamplight."

"Or what?" the first challenged.

There was no reply and the first two sailors laughed.

A man rounded the corner suddenly before I could flee. He was small and wiry with dark hair and a scraggly beard. He paused to see me there and gave me a hard, long look full of menace. Scars ran down the side of his face, tearing through the corner of his mouth, leaving him with a permanent scowl.

I was frozen under that penetrating look.

"You be Beacham's lady," he said suddenly.

I couldn't begin to form an answer.

"You listen to him. You stay off the rail. And you listen to me. You stay in the light."

I nodded, stunned and terrified.

"Ailee?"

I turned to see Grahame hurrying towards me. The gruff sailor pushed past me and didn't look at Grahame as he went.

"Why are you here?" Grahame asked, his voice tense.

I stared at him, my mind blank.

"Come." He took my arm and guided me more brusquely than was his manner. He released me at the passageway. "Go below."

I finally recalled why I had come to find him, but the look he gave me did not encourage me to press him now. I hurried below.

Unsettled and shaking, I made my way to the chicken coop. I couldn't bear the berths where it was too crowded to hear my own thoughts. There were fewer chickens than when we'd set out. Many had gone into the broth Beacham made when we were all so ill. The others clucked softly when I entered, hoping for feed.

I overturned the bucket I used to carry feed to them and sat, my thoughts stumbling over themselves.

What if Beacham's tales weren't just stories? What if they were true?

I never considered it possible. After all, nanny's stories had been just tales.

But what if they weren't?

Fear and excitement buzzed through me in turns. I saw a new world stretch out before me, a world filled with giants and fair folk and creatures rising from the waters to steal unsuspecting sailors. A world where old scarfs held power.

It was nonsense, but for a moment, recalling the look in Rake's eyes, I could believe it was true.

On the day the first ship was sighted, Elsie and I went on deck with the men to see. It was far away and looked so small.

"Brigantine," I heard one of the men say.

"Can you see whose?"

"Need a glass for that."

"Don't need no glass," Beacham said from behind me. "That be a pirate."

A cold silence fell over the group. Elsie raised a hand to her mouth in horror. I, however, felt a small thrill run up my back. I'd spent the last few days retelling Beacham's and nanny's stories to myself, and here was one come to life.

Pirates.

"They sail these waters," Beacham continued, "looking fer treasure ships."

"Then they'll leave us alone," one of the men said, though not entirely certain.

"They have to make sure first," Beacham said. "They'll follow us a time, decide whether to come closer. They've got more sail than we, so they'd catch us up if they wanted."

"What would happen if they did?" I asked. A couple of the men gave me hard looks, and I realized I probably shouldn't be speaking to the cook in open company.

"Depends on their captain. They might sail us past, having a look. They might call out to us. They might fire upon us or try to board us."

"They can't do that!" another man said, indignant.

"Oh, they can, trust in me," Beacham said with his gap-toothed grin. "We'd have seventy men to their hundred and more, unless the lot of you know how to fight. We've four guns to their twenty or more. We're loaded down and riding low and maneuver like a full cart pulled by a lame draft. Oh, they can take us, if they wanted."

"Mr. Beacham!"

The captain's voice pierced the whispers of fear and dread. The captain had come up to the group, and by the look on his face, he'd heard Beacham's speech.

Beacham's face went pale, and he turned toward his captain. He tugged his forelock. "Cap'n, sir."

"Stow that talk and return below."

Beacham gave his forelock another tug and scurried away. By the way the captain watched him go, I had the feeling that Beacham wasn't out of trouble yet.

"He likes to tell stories," I said to Elsie to calm her, but I also said it loud enough that maybe the captain would not be so hard on the cook. "I'm sure we'll be fine."

"That we will, madam," the captain answered. "There is nothing to be concerned. These waters see quite a bit of travel."

"Does that mean we are close?" Mr. Vance asked.

"It does," the captain answered. "With good weather and a fair wind, we shall make land by the week's end."

The attitude in the group changed from fear to hope, and they broke away into twos and threes to discuss plans for arrival.

"You should be below," the captain told Elsie and me in a tone that brooked no refusal.

"Of course," I said with a curtsy. I took Elsie's arm in mine and steered her toward the hatch. I glanced behind, though, to see the captain giving quiet orders to his first mate. Grahame was standing nearby, and his face was set with determination that held a shadow of danger.

Another thrill ran up my back, but I didn't know if it was from the danger of the pirates or the threat my husband promised should they attempt to take the ship or the fact that one of Beacham's stories had actually come to life.

The pirate ship loomed on the horizon for the rest of the day. Talk in the berths bounced between fear of the pirates and joy that our journey was nearing an end. I sat with Elsie, both of us at our knitting. I was still trying to work out the stitches for Beacham's strange scarf while Elsie worked what might become a shawl or a small blanket. We sat in silence, listening to the talk around us. I was never quite certain what to say to Elsie. So many topics were charged with emotion, like the landing and our future, or the past and where we came from. Shipboard life was safe enough, if I kept it to the day's trials, but there was only so much one could say about living on the ship before the topic was exhausted.

I wanted to ask about her knitting, but if it was a blanket for a baby, that might cause Elsie grief to think about having a child without Jacky.

Elsie solved the problem for me.

"What is it you are working?" Elsie asked, finally taking notice of my knitting.

I held it up and watched it unravel again. I'd long given up on the shawl and had spent the better part of a day pulling it out and rewinding the wool into a ball. Considering the weeks I'd been working on something to resemble the strange scarf, I had absolutely nothing to show for it, but I'd never been happier knitting.

"I'm trying to figure out Beacham's scarf," I admitted.

"His scarf?"

"That loop he wears out on deck. The one the German sailor gave him for protection."

Elsie nodded politely, but I could tell that she didn't recall the story.

"Come, I'll show you."

It gave me an excuse to check on Beacham. We set aside our needles and wool, and I led the way to the galley.

The galley was empty. It was strange not to find Beacham in it. I wondered if the captain had called him to his office or room or whatever a captain used to chastise his men.

I wondered if it might be worse than just a talking to.

To hide my fear for Beacham, I found the scarf where it hung near the doorway. "This is it," I said. I didn't want to touch it while Beacham was gone.

Elsie peered closer at it. "It is a strange stitch." She pulled at it, gently, to spread the garment. "I don't think I've ever seen it's like."

I was a bit disappointed. It would have been nice to find someone who recognized it and could teach me.

"I don't think it's knitting, though," Elsie told me.

"How can you tell?"

"It doesn't look it. The stitches are too . . . different. I wonder, though."

I was about to press her when Beacham stepped to the doorway.

"What's this then? Having at my things?" His tone was hard, and there was a dark light in his eyes.

"I was hoping Elsie might know the stitch," I said quickly as Elsie stepped back from the scarf. "That I could make you another."

Beacham's hard look grew guilty. "I'm sorry, miss. That is kind of ye. I were just—"

"I am sorry we intruded," I interrupted him. "Is there something we can do to help prepare for supper?"

Beacham looked uncertain, then drew himself up. "Well, if ye be offering, I can't see no harm in that."

He set us to the potatoes again, but I didn't protest. I hoped Beacham would speak of what happened with the captain, but he was oddly quiet and reserved as we worked. Elsie seemed no more inclined to speak, which left me to my thoughts, which naturally turned toward pirates. Were they still following us? How would we know if they choose to attack? What would Grahame look like with a musket at his shoulder?

Could I learn to work one, too?

The talk during supper was of the pirates. Most of the men stayed topside, which concerned many of their wives.

"There's naught to be done," Iona said loudly. "Why they think they'll be of any use is beyond me."

"It gives them a sense of duty to be watchful," Tavey told her. "In case something does occur."

"It gives me a headache how much they look to their 'duty' and leave us to the cleaning," Iona grumbled.

"Do you think we should be afraid?" Elsie asked me quietly.

"I can't say," I admitted. Beacham hadn't spoken more than a handful of words to us, and I hadn't been able to tell if his reticence was from concern of the pirates or whatever had happened between him and the captain.

"I can't seem to bring myself to fear," Elsie admitted quietly. "I know I should. The others are, even Iona, though she hides it under anger. But I can't." She looked at me with wide eyes. "Is there something wrong with me?"

I hesitated, uncertain what to say. I wanted to wave off Elsie's concern, but I recalled that time before marrying Grahame when fear lived so close at hand that it became a part of me.

"No, I don't think there's anything wrong with you," I said. "You've lost something irreplaceable. Not just Jacky, though I know that is awful enough. You have a future you can't see into yet." I took Elsie's hand. "But you'll see it again. It can't lie empty forever."

"Do you see yours now?"

I gripped harder. Elsie understood my own struggle, and it meant the world that she did.

"Not yet. But I know it will come."

By morning, the pirate ship had gone. I was somewhat disappointed, but the relief in the berths was palpable. The fear that colored yesterday's talk changed to hope as we drew closer and closer to land. I crept out to the deck often throughout the day to see if land or more pirates had been sighted. Once, Grahame caught me, but he merely gave me that long look of his that had me turning back into the passageway.

As the time for making port came closer, I found that I was beginning to think about leaving the ship. I realized with a shock that I hadn't let myself think about life after landing. My entire focus had been on the ship, surviving the passage, peeling yet another wizened old potato, making another stitch. I'd considered Elsie's future, worried over it and tried to imagine what it might be like for her once we arrived, but I'd never given much thought to my own.

Now that I was, I found that I couldn't imagine what it would be like at all. I didn't have any stories of the new world. I wanted to talk to Elsie about it, but I was afraid that would only bring up dark thoughts for her. Tavey was too busy for more than a passing exchange. Iona was too good at seeing only the bad that could happen. And I hadn't gotten to know most of the other women.

So I asked Beacham.

"You said you've been to the new world before," I began, leaning in the galley doorway.

"To the West Indies, that I have." He glanced over at me from where he was chopping yet more salt beef. "But that weren't nothing like where we be heading, miss, if you're wanting to know."

"Have you spoken to anyone who has been where we're heading?" I thought the port was called Fillydelfy, but I wasn't certain. I'd heard the name bantered back and forth in the berths several times, but the pronunciation kept changing.

"Oh, a few. One of the crew has been afore he joined this ship."

"Truly!"

"But don't you go running off to find him," Beacham warned. "I'm sure

66

your man has already spoken with him."

I was both excited and disappointed. I wondered if he meant Rakes. I didn't see the harm in asking.

"Was it Mr. Rakes?"

Beacham froze, then he slowly looked at me, the light in his eyes a dangerous glimmer.

"What know ye of Rakes?" he asked in a hushed tone.

"I . . . I overheard him on deck," I stammered, taken aback.

"Ye keep away from Rakes," Beacham told me. "That man be scarred by more than what mars his face."

"What do you mean?"

"Just keep away from him."

"He told me—" I hesitated under Beacham's glare. "He told me to listen to you. To stay off the rail."

Beacham turned back to his chopping board. "Ye should be back in the berths, miss." His voice was still hushed.

"Mr. Beacham—"

"Good day, miss."

I held back a sigh, dismayed. Returning to the berths, I found Elsie at my cot.

"I was looking for you," she said.

"I was seeing if Mr. Beacham needed help." What had I done to put him off so? What was it about Rakes that fretted him?

"I had a thought," Elsie told me. "Do you know this?" She held out the kerchief she had first worn to board the ship. "This lace, here."

I nodded. "Cheyne lace. I have a shawl worked with it."

Elsie looked impressed. "Truly? Well, my thought was that something like this made Mr. Beacham's scarf. But in wool, not thread. I've never seen it done quite that way, it might be a stitch I wasn't taught."

"Do you think it possible?"

"It might be. Though I'm not sure what tool you would use. When I do cheyne lace, I use a needle of sorts."

"You know how to make cheyne lace?"

Elsie nodded, looking embarrassed. "My mother taught me. She used to make it to sell, before she wed my father."

"Could you teach me?"

Elsie frowned with a pained expression. "My tools are in the hold. But perhaps when we make land . . ." Her words trailed off.

When we make land, neither of us knew what to expect.

I wasn't going to think about it. "That would be wonderful," I told her, smiling. My answer pleased her, easing the pain from her face. We sat and looked over the lace on her kerchief and she spoke of her mother's work. All I could think about was my shawl nestled in the bottom of my bag and, though I knew it unlikely, wonder if Elsie's mother had made it.

That evening, Grahame took his supper in the berths. It was an odd sight, him sitting on a stool in the narrow space, bent over like a giant in a child's room. I'd stopped taking him his meals after my illness since I'd been so busy helping with Elsie and the others. I'd offered once, but he'd gestured to where Beacham was handing out the crew member's meals and that had been that. Usually I took my meals with Elsie.

This evening, though, he sat with me. I felt as nervous as when we'd taken our first meal together as husband and wife. I didn't know what to say or where to look. The food had gotten plainer and more predictable, but I ate it because there was nothing else. I was sick to death of potatoes and peas and salt beef and those hard little biscuits.

"When we make land, we'll take a room," Grahame said, surprising me.

"Where?"

"In town."

I watched him, no longer interested in my own meal, hoping he would speak more of his plans. He cleaned off his plate with the appetite of a working man.

"We'll see land soon," he told me. "It will be days yet to make port."

He was offering me that information to warn me, I realized. I nodded, to show I understood.

He handed me his empty trencher. Before he left, though, he leaned towards me.

"You've done well," he said in a hushed tone. It was as though he was surprised by the fact.

I didn't know how to feel about that, and he didn't give me time to respond. I watched him disappear up the passage.

The next day we sighted land.

Everyone went topside to see it. The green was a solid strip along the horizon cutting the ocean and sky in two. It had been so long since I'd seen land, or seen such green, that I cried. I wasn't alone in my tears. Elsie clung to me, holding in sobs, and I knew she was crying for more than the sight of land.

The passengers remained on deck for a long while, watching that strip of land. Some of the joyful murmurings began to sour as the strip grew no larger.

"Grahame says it'll be a few days before we make port," I told Elsie.

"How many?"

"I'm not sure."

A few others overheard me and the news spread quickly. Most of the passengers returned below, but Elsie and I remained on deck, standing on the forecastle clutching one another in the cold wind, staring landward.

With a sudden impulse, I asked Elsie to wait while I dashed below deck. I returned with the wedding shawl folded in my arms.

"I want you to have this," I told her, pressing the shawl into Elsie's arms.

Elsie breathed out in wonder. "I can't take this," she argued.

"Yes, you can." I stepped back, crossing my arms. "You need something lovely to look on, something of beauty and home and friendship. You keep that and maybe it'll help remind you that you aren't alone. Then you give it to your baby, if it's a girl, and tell her of our homeland and her father and of me. And if it's a boy, do the same. He'll have a fine gift for a future wife.

"But if things go wrong, you sell it," I insisted. My eyes were brimming with tears, and Elsie was weeping quietly. "You use it to keep yourself and your babe. It's my gift to you, and don't you hesitate to use it, Elsie MacClayne."

Elsie embraced me, clutching me tightly. The grief struck me like a blow that I would be parted from my dearest friend. I tried for a moment to contain it, but I hadn't the strength. We wept, the shawl pressed between us.

I wasn't sure how long we huddled together, overcome, but when I finally regained control, my eyes were sore and puffy. I found my handkerchief and dabbed at my nose.

"We can do this," Elsie told me. Her face was resolute, even with tears still gleaming in the sunlight. She gripped my hand.

I took a steadying breath. "We can do this."

How, I had no idea, but I intended to try. Like it or not, the new world was waiting for us both. I didn't know where my path would take me, except away from Elsie, but I knew I wouldn't be completely alone. Grahame would be there, and I wanted to trust in him. I wasn't entirely certain that I did, yet, but I was beginning to. More importantly, I was beginning to trust in myself.

The rest would have to take care of itself.

And I'll stay away from the rail, I thought, smiling through my tears as Elsie and I gazed out over the green strip of land on the horizon.

It was a start.

To be continued in *Unraveling: The New World, Part Two*

Available from Ficstitches Yarns Crochet Kit Club
Included in Kit Number 2, On Sale in July, 2015

Please visit ficstitchesyarns.com for more information

Thank you for reading!

ABOUT THE AUTHOR

C. Jane Reid is a writer, poet, and blogger. She holds a Bachelor of Arts in both Literature and History and completed a Master's degree in Literature with a novel focused on WWI poet, Alan Seeger. A lifelong writer, she is excited to combine her interest in history with her love for crochet in a series of crochet stories influenced by historical events, romance, and a touch of the paranormal. She lives in the Pacific Northwest with her husband, daughter, son, and Kiwi, the laziest cat in the world.

24717665R00046

Made in the USA
San Bernardino, CA
03 October 2015